Jack Carnegie

The Auschwitz Protocol

Copyright © 2020 by Jack Carnegie

The right of Jack Carnegie to be identified as the author of this work has been asserted in accordance with the Copyright, Designs and Patents Act 1988.

All rights reserved.

This book or any portion thereof may not be reproduced or used in any manner whatsoever without the express written permission of the author.

This is a work of fiction.

Names, characters, places, organisations, events and incidents are either the products of the author's imagination or are used fictitiously. Any resemblance to actual persons, living or dead, businesses, companies, events, or locales is entirely coincidental.

ISBN: 9798471891944

Cover by Jack Carnegie

Acknowledgements
Paul Addy, without whom this book
would not be what it is.

To Carol for all she does, keeping me happy
is not an easy job but it's natural to her
and then there is Max, who is my inspiration,
a beautiful little man and the best dog in the world.

Chapter 1

Auschwitz Birkenau

My return to Auschwitz Birkenau was in the December of 1993. It was a short weekend break and I'd told my wife Luiza we'd visit the Wieliczka Salt Mines on the outskirts of Krakow. She was oblivious to the mark on my left lower arm where I'd removed the six numbers I'd been tattooed with all those years earlier.

I'd received it in 1943 in Auschwitz 1, just before my transfer to Birkenau (Auschwitz 2) and my serial number was 104627; underneath was a triangle representing I was a Jew.

I took it off with a knife, physically cutting the mark from my skin. It healed leaving a small scar and, as it did so, I'd deliberately picked and re-picked the wound to ensure the numbers never came back.

As we entered through the gates, we were met by the words 'Arbeit Macht Frei'. They were words well known to me; 'Work sets you free' and in my thoughts were the many who didn't get to see their freedom.

A sadness filled me and my head hung low but I was with Luiza so I pulled myself together. I'd come after many years of denying I'd ever been incarcerated in the camps. I had a mission to fulfil and I'd sworn to myself that before I died my story would be heard, but I had to remember everything, all the terrors and all of the nightmares that had been Auschwitz Birkenau.

Above me was the metal arch made by the order of the camp commandant, Rudolf Höss. Made by prisoners with metalwork skills, the slogan it bore was used by the Nazis at the entrance of a number of concentration camps; an insult to the many who perished at their hands, words that betrayed.

Höss would not have thought the words mere mockery, more likely a promise that those who were worked into an early grave would eventually find some form of 'freedom'.

We walked around the site until I came upon the first gas chamber. Across a small patch of grass stood the hangman's gallows. It was here that SS Obersturmbannfuhrer Höss met his death, after being sentenced by a Polish court. They hung him on a short rope.

He'd studied extermination methods, testing and perfecting the techniques of mass murder, and introduced to the killing process Zyklon B, hydrogen cyanide, thus enabling his soldiers to efficiently murder up to two thousand people an hour and making it the chosen instrument of death in their 'Final Solution'.

Here I was, standing where he died, the man who organised all this death. The silence all around me was invasive. Although many people were visiting, there was a stillness to the place, a shame. I held Luiza's hand whilst I kept myself together. I couldn't let her see my upset, although, it would be perfectly understandable for anyone visiting this site of mass killing to show some sadness. I guarded my feelings and emotions carefully.

Block 15 housed the historical introduction to the site and blocks four to seven had been converted from barracks to a museum. Luiza was uncomfortable in here, especially block 5 inside which we found the shoes and a plaque stating they were forty-three thousand pairs. What stood out were a little girl's red shoes. Somehow, because of the color, you were drawn to them. All the others seemed to have faded, over time, to a deathly grey but the red remained, focusing the mind; a little girl's feet once fitted inside these shoes and they had coldly, efficiently, and as a part of a system, killed her.

Luiza wiped tears from her eyes. "How could they?" This, I wasn't expecting, it drew me into an awkward conversation so I squeezed her hand in an effort to quell her upset and we moved on through, past the window showing hundreds and hundreds of suitcases, names scrawled over them in the vain hope they would be returned; others bore the word 'Waisenkind' – orphan. The trust placed in their murderers tightened the fist around my heart.

Artificial legs and crutches filled the next display and the hair of some 140,000 victims of the camp filled the following. It had been cut from the heads of women and little girls after they had been gassed. They'd shaved the heads of dead people and used it as a 'product' to make mattress filling, cloth and socks.

Blue and grey striped uniforms in block 6 brought back memories. Flashbacks came to me which I didn't care much for but I had to endure. I recalled being in this very building as a new entrant when it was a barracks, barefooted and cold, clothes hanging off me. I blinked the thoughts away and concentrated; I couldn't allow myself to be overcome.

I made my excuses to Luiza, I'd have to take some fresh air. She nodded and said, "Don't be long, Emil." I walked from the room, turning a corner just as my emotion burst from my chest. Holding my forehead, I gasped for air, oxygen seemed hard to come by. It was more of a shock than I had assumed it was going to be but I was determined to see it through.

I returned to Luiza, who seemed preoccupied with something or other. She asked me if I was alright. I lied and said yes, she held my hand in comfort, holding it close to her heart.

We walked to block 10. I knew this block. They experimented on people there; for the most part they were mainly women. I was taken there one day with another. We were to remove some tables and were told to wait in the hall. The screams I heard were awful. It was a place from hell, feared by us all.

After walking out of block 10 with a feeling of nausea from deep within and memories recalled that I didn't really want to remember, I asked Luiza if she was alright. Her response was a terse "No, not really!" I comforted her and we walked towards the exit as I told her, "It wasn't a visit to enjoy but one to remember." She agreed and said she was sorry for being abrupt; it had been a shock, all that we had seen.

"Why have you brought me here, Emil?" she asked and I dithered a little in my response. "Krakow is such a beautiful city, it would be rude not to visit and pay our respects to the fallen of the holocaust." I hoped she'd accept my explanation, thankfully she did. "Yes, you're right, Emil," she replied, quietly.

We continued towards the exit, Luiza had seen enough but I was disappointed to leave as I hadn't seen what I wanted to see, the photographs I'd heard of, somewhere on the Auschwitz site there was a wall full of photographs. I'd planned the visit to take in the faces of my past, to maybe recognise people and to find out their fate.

We walked to the small shop looking for water and a boy brought two small bottles from under the counter. I handed Luiza one and passed him ten zloty. We drank from the bottles which seemed to steady both of us, flushing out the poison running through our veins like an infection. Our walk around the site seemed to be slowly greying our bones yet I was glad we came. I would take on board what I'd seen and, somehow, I'd find a way to see the photographs I'd sought.

Most importantly to me, Luiza had not suspected anything and I hadn't let myself down which I'd been worried about. We joined the coach we'd arrived on and, whilst we waited for the others on our tour, Luiza talked of visiting the jazz club in Krakow. Rumour had it Nigel Kennedy the violinist played there, actually he lived above the club, and she was a great fan of his.

We planned some lunch in the town, a traditional polish stew we'd looked forward so much to, but small talk wasn't where my head was right at that moment. My thoughts returned to my memories as I looked out over the site I once was a part of. I'd have to try to return without Luiza, I couldn't make her suffer for my needs.

As the coach pulled away, I looked back and an odd feeling of emptiness came over me, possibly because I'd not got what I came for but more likely because I was looking at the site of so many deaths. Perhaps the dead were reaching out and trying to drag me back.

Towards Krakow town, my mind wandered. I had to find out if they were still alive and what had happened in the years in between.

Had they had a good life or had the demons destroyed them? These were the thoughts that had filled my mind ever since I found out they were on the wall of 'Life of the Prisoners' in the museum.

Luiza pulled me from my speculation. "It was awful to see the human cost of war. How could they hate so much?" she asked. "I don't know sweetheart, it's such a terrible thing to see," I said with a nervous heart. I'd known it would be difficult bringing her to the camp. I had expectations of failure and letting my feelings and emotions overtake me, forcing me to open up, which would have been the wrong thing to do at the time. She would know, when the time was right

We were dropped off in the center and said farewells to the group then decided to seek out the Polish stew we'd planned. Later that night, we did indeed go to the jazz club and Nigel Kennedy entertained us for a few hours playing with a jazz-rock quintet.

We'd booked the Hotel Rezydent and it was beautiful, the room, finely decorated, came with an en suite bathroom. I'd got it through a broker in Greenwich and the cost was minimal, there was a good exchange rate at the time, I recall.

Sleep that night was hard to come by, my mind raced and I tossed and turned until, eventually, exhaustion took me away.

The following morning, I woke to the sound of the telephone ringing, I must have dropped off around 5 am, it was the morning call we'd requested from reception. "Morning sir, this is your wake-up call," came down the line. I thanked him, replaced the receiver and checked my watch. "Oh, just half an hour more," Luiza begged. "If we do that we'll miss breakfast," I responded. "Oh ok," she reluctantly replied. We showered, dressed and descended the stairs, all the while my mind occupied by the letter.

We'd endured the procedures and system of rule the SS and the Kapos subjected us to simply to stay alive and it haunted me. I'd been a police officer in the Policja until 1939 when all hell broke loose with the outbreak of the war. I was a fit young man, nineteen years of age, the world was my oyster and I had dreams like any other young Polish boy. The Germans changed all that.

Up until 1955, I'd spent years in recovery after what I'd been through and it took all my strength to return to the person I was before, both mentally and physically. I'd lived my life until I met Luiza, that same year, as a troubled soul, a victim of hate, but when I met her my life changed, it blossomed, so much so I was able to put my previous life to sleep and attempt to forget what I'd been through.

Now it seemed it was only a temporary hibernation. I was destined to finish what had been started all those years ago, justice had to be served.

Luiza and I visited the salt mines at Wieliczka and lit a candle in memory of the victims of the Holocaust. It was an extraordinary experience. The Chapel of St Kinga was the most impressive of all, hand carved from the salt in the mine, the whole thing was a wonder to see. At seven hundred years of age, the mine was, as the guide told us, the oldest Polish company.

For a while, I forgot about the camp, my mind was distracted by the sights and beauty around me but, as Luiza lit the candle, I once again returned to it in my thoughts.

The letter I'd received some three weeks earlier played on my mind, it was addressed to me and signed off by an 'Aleksy Markowski', a name not familiar to me. Within, it explained six people were on Auschwitz's 'The Life Of Prisoners' wall that should not be there.

They were Kapos, displayed as supposedly normal prisoners, their photographs placed on the wall as having died in the gas chambers, but they hadn't. Somehow, they'd escaped liberation by the Soviets and were seemingly alive and well. Further reading told me the intention; the rules the Kapos had lived by would be used to capture and punish them, they would be their downfall. Lukas Baur, an Austrian block leader, would be the first.

The position of 'Kapo' was given by the SS. They were prisoners themselves and they'd supervise work details and daily living, often dealing out beatings or worse – collaborators who brutally forced the other prisoners, whether they were sick or starving, to hard labour and, frequently, close to death.

They were often violent criminals, more brutal than the SS, as their position depended on the guards' satisfaction. I had first-hand knowledge of many Kapos. I recalled the beatings I'd taken from my block leader when I first entered Auschwitz and a shudder went through me. There were, of course, one or two decent Kapos who tried to help with food or easier work details but they were the exception, the rest of them were selfish, only interested in saving themselves.

There were three levels of Kapo: camp leaders, block leaders and room leaders. For some it wasn't just self-survival, some began to view it as a career and they would do whatever it took to ingratiate themselves with any SS man who could further their aims.

Upon liberation, some of them were beaten and killed for their crimes, by fellow prisoners. Despised for what they'd done; they were given swift justice. The ones who survived found themselves on trial in a post-war world; most would be sentenced to life, some to a death sentence.

I couldn't ignore the fact that from all the people who'd survived Auschwitz, I'd been chosen by Aleksy Markowski, whoever *he* was, to identify the missing Kapos and bring them to justice and the letter shocked me when it arrived out of the blue. Addressing me quite personally, it named me by my full name and seemed to be from a person that had known me either in the ghetto or within Auschwitz. Maybe he was a prisoner himself; Markowski had my attention.

I'd decided straight away to book the weekend break as an initial focal point of the project ahead of me and I'd use the information I'd received in the letter, the name given and also Markowski himself.

A return address was given as the Hotel San Georgio, Naples, Italy. I phoned them and asked after him several times but was told he wasn't available. I left my number and waited for him to call back. On the run-up to the weekend break to Krakow, I'd heard nothing so we took the trip anyway.

Luiza enjoyed the remainder of the holiday, we made the most of the city, it was cold but we were well wrapped up and a few shots of vodka helped keep the chill away. The opportunity to return to the camp did not materialise.

Our return flight to JFK was another ten and a half hours leaving Krakow mid-afternoon and arriving early evening. Our son, Daniel, was at the airport to pick us up. Born in '66, he was brought up in a peaceful household and, at that time of our life, we'd chosen to settle into our home in Idar Court. A beautiful boy who'd always made us proud. His sister Lena was a year younger but you wouldn't know it, she always *was* the older of the two. They both lived close by, had partners and fussed over us terribly. Lena would be at our home making sure we had a meal to eat after our long journey.

As I entered the house, Max, our black Labrador, performed his usual greeting by picking a slipper up in his mouth and excitedly offering it as a welcome gift, his face alight with enjoyment as his tail wagged so much his rear end swayed from side to side. He was a good boy, a full breed with the strong, wide shoulders such hunting dogs were known for and his adoration for his mother, Luiza, was obvious to see; a real character in our house who everyone loved.

Before buying Max as a pup, I'd had the opportunity to buy an Alsatian but resisted because of my memories of Auschwitz. They'd used those dogs to tear prisoners apart and the memory of that was just too much for me to have one as a pet.

I noticed the answerphone had messages but decided to take them the next morning; it had been a long hard day.

We slept well that night, the long journey took its toll on us and we fell easily into a deep sleep, waking only once in the night to let Max out. I woke before Luiza and put a pot of coffee on. Looking over at the answerphone, I remembered the messages.

I pressed the play button and the machine leapt into action. "Hello, this is Aleksy Markowski, I'm returning your call. I can meet you in the coffee house in the 'Bruce Museum' on the 23rd at 11 am. Don't worry, I'll identify myself but I know who you are." The answerphone clicked as it ended the call. Stood for a while wondering, I grabbed a piece of paper, wrote down what the message had told me and pressed delete.

No need to worry Luiza yet, she didn't deserve any of this. What was going to happen was unknown but I felt duty-bound and compelled to listen to what Aleksy Markowski had to say.

The days ahead were a complete blur to me, I had only one thing on my mind and that was the meeting. What would he tell me and what did he know of the men he would name? Most importantly, why now, all these years later? The world didn't seem interested anymore. These were answers I'd get from the meeting, along with many others from the questions I'd collated since I received the letter.

Time seemed to drag between our trip to Krakow and the 23rd and my curiosity ran wild. I also felt nervous for reasons of my own. Luiza and I very rarely spent time apart so I'd have to make something up so she wouldn't want to come with me. I felt like I was betraying her by lying, but it was all in the cause. I'd tell her I was meeting an old friend, someone she didn't know and tell her it would only be for a few hours.

When the day arrived, I was up early. I'd been playing Karl Jenkins 'The Armed Man' when the track 'Benedictus' came on. It brought a tear to my eye as I thought of all those poor souls walking into the gas chambers. It was a beautiful piece of music that made your heart pound with emotion, the cello pulling away at your soul. Coincidence? Maybe subconsciously I'd put it on knowing I needed to feel pity for those lost souls of Auschwitz.

Classical music was in both our hearts, we had a collection of music of all genres but classical was a joint love and Karl Jenkins certainly a favourite.

As I said goodbye to Luiza, my nerves took a hold of me. I didn't know what to expect and, for a moment, it crossed my mind not to go, but as fast as it came to me, it departed. I'd dressed smartly, I don't know why, I guess it felt like an interview or that I should be respectful to Markowski or something along those lines.

Passing the harbour, the Bruce Museum was a fifteen-minute walk from home. It was a fine day, the sun was out and there were dead leaves on the ground. It could almost have been the Fall.

I arrived at the coffee shop a little early, bought a cappuccino and drank it whilst sitting outside, taking in the beauty of the day. I'd been humming 'Benedictus' on my way and still had the cello in my thoughts as I sat waiting.

"Hello, I'm Aleksy. Shall we go inside?" a man in an electric wheelchair said. I jumped up and held the door open for him to pass through and we found an area nearby where we could talk. I got two coffees.

He started the conversation. "I'll be as straight as I can be. I know about you so let's not waste any time. You were in Auschwitz when these men were." He placed a thin folder on the table. "As you can see, I'm wheelchair bound. I have a deteriorating condition they call motor neurone disease and it means I will get worse as time goes on. I started my work on this way back in 1961 when I received papers from the Israeli intelligence service who were working on the Eichmann case." He paused briefly, watching me take in what he was saying.

"It has taken me years to identify and hunt down these men but two years ago I developed my illness. I intend to hand over to you the continuation of my work, one case at a time. You'll get a file with all that is known about the subject. You will seek out, identify and denounce them, *but* it's essential the police wait for the others to be identified before any arrests are made as it will make news headlines around the world when announced and we do not want any one of these people going into hiding," he said, as if knowing I was going to take on the case.

I tried to argue. "Hang on a minute, this was fifty-five years ago, another life, why would I do this?"

He ignored my question. "The files will be given to you one at a time. I cannot trust a life's work to a single individual and I will assess you as we go on." Anticipating my question of who'd be paying for all this, he continued, "You'll be given expenses for accommodation, travel and also for your meals, anything else you'll need to request as you go along." His determination was clear, he wasn't going to take no for an answer.

"Here is file number one. Collaborator and registered criminal Lukas Baur, a Kapo block leader you will know from your time in the camp. This man was responsible for beating a man to death, he assisted the SS in the hanging of twelve Latvian Jews and even personally volunteered to place canisters of Zyklon B in the funnels of the gas chambers in which thousands died.

"He avoided justice along with the others by escaping hours before the liberation of the camp; he knew his offences would mean certain death once he was identified to the Soviet liberators. Your job is to bring this man to trial and to get justice for his victims," he pronounced.

I sat back in my chair, taking it all in. "This is going to impact on my wife and my children," I said, in a hope I knew was futile.

He gave me a thin smile. "They will understand, now take the file and look after its contents, there's a life's work inside."

Startling me, his wheelchair shifted backwards abruptly, swivelled and headed towards the exit and I automatically jumped up to open the door for him.

"My number is on a card in the file, it's a mobile number, save it to your phone and I'll be in touch," he said.

"I don't own a mobile," I replied.

"Then get one," he said with a cursory glance and off he went leaving me with this huge burden, one he'd carried for thirty years, one I must now explain to my unsuspecting wife.

The walk home was not one I enjoyed. The file tucked safely inside my coat, I pondered how on earth I was going to tell Luiza. She would not understand any of this, it would be too much for her to handle at her age.

We'd been retired for the past eight years, I was seventy-three years old and my police life was behind me. Luiza was five years younger and had been a midwife until the pension beckoned. She'd taken to retirement with the enthusiasm of a young woman, she would not take to this, this would be hard for her.

I walked slowly, recalling what had been said; a collaborator I'd known in the camp whose brutality was feared *and* the beating Markowski mentioned was one I'd not forget, not in a lifetime.

In 1943, a weakened malnourished man was struggling and Baur beat him with a thick, rudimentary truncheon, a simple long shaft of wood maybe two feet in length. Beatings were commonplace place in Auschwitz, but this one caused the death of a man, hit about the head so badly his skull had cracked open and brain matter oozed out. Baur continued the beating, even after death he frenziedly attacked the corpse.

The man had done nothing but have his body fail on him because of the starvation he'd endured. An SS officer watched as the Kapo executed him, Baur's eyes drawn to the unspoken encouragement. As blood and brains seeped out into the mud, I remember thinking, *will he feel the final strikes when death comes* but neither of us had to suffer much longer, which was a blessing. Yes, I remembered the beating, it had never gone away.

I stopped at the bay, looked out over Greenwich harbour and wept. This was a life I'd hidden. I'd started a new one in '55. How had it caught up with me? The man in my head screamed.

My walk back was troubling, would Luiza support me? I'd spent my life lying about my past but I'd just wanted to put it behind me; I'd been through so much, the only thing I could do was to pretend it didn't happen. I feared it being a part of my life because it was so horrendous. It was me that had been through it and it was me that had to decide how to deal with it. I believed I'd done what most victims of the holocaust had done – put it in a box, locked it in a cupboard and thrown away the key. Now, someone had returned it.

I walked into the house to be greeted by Max and the slipper, Luiza was next. "How did your meeting go, Emil?" she enquired from the top of the stairs.

"Yes, very good, we had coffee," I grabbed for a response.

"What did you talk about?" she persisted.

"Oh we talked of the children mostly and Max," I lied.

"Emil Janowitz, you're not telling me everything, you're keeping secrets and Luiza will get them out of you," she toyed with me, not realising the awful truth.

"No, no Luiza I'm not." Then I quickly changed the subject. "Would you like a cup of tea? Has Max been walked?" I was trying to fill a void and occupy her mind before she could come back with more enquiries. "Has the paper been delivered?" I continued in the hope she'd lose her train of thought.

"Yes, I'd love a cup of tea. Yes, Max has been walked and yes, it's on the table in the hall," she responded, sarcastically.

She came down the stairs and slowly walked up to me. "Emil, tell me. Something troubles you. I've known you for nearly forty years and you cannot disguise things from me. I'm your wife. What's wrong?"

I knew it was over, it was time. "Sit down, Luiza, I've something to tell you, something you won't like."

Chapter 2
The Warsaw Ghetto

The Warsaw ghetto was the largest of all ghettos in German occupied Europe, over 400,000 people were imprisoned there at one point. Averaging nine people per room, it was a difficult existence but we somehow found a way to live as a family.

In our room, my father, mother, sister, brother and grandparents lived along with two of our neighbours who had moved in when conditions with the people next door had become intolerable.

My father was a chemist and well respected in the neighbourhood of my childhood and would continue his work within the ghetto as best he could. Mother had helped in the shop, distributing the prescriptions he dealt out, and it was often unnecessary for him to get involved in the diagnosis of the patient, such was her gift. As children, we thought she healed people by talking to them.

My parents, Antoni and Zofia, were married in 1918 just after the First World War and Papa served in the 1st Rifle Division in 1919, seeing quite extensive action in the Polish-Bolshevik War.

My grandparents, Kacper and Alicja, had supported the January uprising of 1863 but the rebellion had eventually failed when the rebel forces were severely outnumbered by the Russians. They were fortunate to evade the awful reprisals that followed.

Before the roundup, my younger brother, Filip, wanted to follow me into the Policja; at just 16 he had the world at his feet. He was a clever boy whose looks made him popular with the girls and he accepted their attention as a gift from above which often caused trouble for Papa.

My sister was the baby of the family. Only 7 years of age, Anna found it hard in the ghetto because she'd only ever known our home in Luborzyca which had been idyllic in comparison to the conditions we now found ourselves having to get used to.

Our neighbours, originally from the next room, were Tomasz and Kinga Fogel. She was named after the saint worshipped in the salt mines. Nice people with whom we'd struck up a friendship, they were from Skawina. Everyone pulled their weight, each doing a part of a whole that only they could do. It had to be that way because rationing was strict. However, it didn't take long for us to realise there was never going to be enough to sustain us.

When we had sold everything we didn't absolutely need in order to buy goods on the black market, Filip and I knew we'd have to do something more. The high mindedness of a former policeman and his hopeful recruit had to be thrown out of the window and, through a few contacts we'd made when bartering, we joined the ranks of the smugglers.

People were dying around us: men, women and children, old and young. If you had nothing to barter or sell when you came into the ghetto, you wouldn't last long. The council of elders sanctioned the setting up of soup kitchens for the less fortunate but all they really did was prolong the inevitable. At best 150 calories a meal, they could only prepare people for death.

It wasn't a good thing to stand out in a crowd, so we restricted ourselves to simply trying to maintain a reasonable level of health whilst attempting to help as many others as was possible. Some of our neighbours volunteered for resettlement in the east, often tempted by the promise of extra rations of bread and jam. They waved goodbye and shouted they would send us word of their new lives. We heard nothing. New people came in, we had to be careful.

As a family, there was plenty of love in our household, not often spoken about but it was fundamental. Respect and trust were all a big part of our family and it was knitted together by love for each other.

Our sister, little Anna, was the central focus for my brother and I and we fussed over her. She demanded your attention as children do but she was cute with it so it was fun for us both to join in whatever it was she was grabbing your attention for.

I guess I'd done the same with Filip when he was a youngster but his time had passed when Anna was born; at nine years old, he grew up quickly. From that age, he really became an individual and not so needing of us, of me. Now, we both shared the joy of seeing our little sister grow up – she was a blessing.

Our mother, father and grandparents could see the love both Filip and I had for her. You could see the pleasure they took in seeing their children play and you'd often catch them glancing at each and smiling when Filip was playing chequers with her – a game we'd made from buttons and a piece of card.

He'd often, if not always, allow little Anna to win, cupping his hands to his face upon the final move and declaring with amazement, "Oh my word, how do you do it?" to which she would say words to the effect of "I'm just fantastic am I not", her eyes wide open, which made the whole family laugh with joy. Her smile could melt you.

We'd each take turns telling, as we called it, 'ni night' stories to Anna and we'd often get her to read the first chapter of whatever book we had at the time and then take over until she fell asleep or told us, "Alright, I'm ok now. You can stop."

She was a very beautiful child and we all loved her dearly. You could tell our parents were proud of us by the way they took a step back, denying themselves the pleasures of teaching her in order to get the greater enjoyment of seeing their sons do it.

My brother's determination to help us get through the ghetto was nothing more than inspiring, as little a thing as it seemed. He once brought two apples home one day, one each for Kacper and Alicja, our grandparents, as a gift. They were so pleased and thankful they completely forgot they had no teeth to eat them with. "The greatest present any man could wish for," my grandfather declared. "So beautiful a gift, I'd feel guilty eating it," 'Babcia' said, words without realisation.

I don't recall what happened to those apples but I always remembered with fondness imagining them both sitting in their chairs, sucking away at them. It was an image that would stay with me and every time I thought of my grandparents, a smile would come across my face.

I'd watched my parents as Filip gave these gifts to my grandparents and when my mother was just about to say the obvious, father nudged her, keeping her quiet and she turned away disguising a smile. Later, she'd scold him, "You should have said something", but neither grandparent was any the wiser nor indeed was Filip, for a streetwise kid sometimes he had a complete innocence.

Perhaps their innocence made us love them, the quintessential childlike element to them that made them the people they were.

My grandfather would often tell stories of his youth, he was very proud of his country and all that his generation had done in his days. He would always follow by saying how very proud he was of Papa, instilling a pride in us of our father, and then he'd touch each one of our cheeks saying, "*And* you children, so very, very proud. You're so beautiful. Your mama and papa are blessed by you, you are very special children."

He was a great man who, along with our grandmother, had created a wonderful family. I would often think about other families, did they have what we had ? I hoped they did.

My grandmother was like my grandfather's stooge, she'd often wink and make faces behind his back when he was telling us what to do or giving orders but he'd always catch her, which I'm sure was meant. She'd burst out laughing, "Do this, Do that, blah blah blah" and mock him, pulling a face whilst we laughed.

He'd look stern and then break down laughing at himself. That was my grandparents, they were not strict nor unloving, they would tell us often how precious we were to them.

I can't tell you what that meant at the time but it certainly made us feel special and loved; even at 19 years of age I felt that love, I was never too big for a cuddle off my grandmother or a hug from my grandfather.

Our daily battle with survival took a turn for the worse in March of that year when food got so scarce we really were struggling to put a meal on the table.

We didn't know our parents fed us having foregone their own for our sake, saying they'd had their meal earlier. That went on for a while until our grandparents both took ill, their immune systems were run down and that winter was bitter cold. Without nourishment, they went down hill really quickly. I remember my father praying at night for the lives of his parents. It shocked me and from that moment I realised how precious life was, it could be taken away at the blink of an eye.

So Filip and I did what we did best but we did it better. We bartered, we scrounged, we stole and we survived through the ghetto and brought food home to our family.

It was hard, harder than imaginable, we'd be out all day working. Tiredness would overtake both of us and being malnourished didn't help but it was purely overwork that eventually made me ill. I came down with shingles, a nasty nerve damaging illness that left open cuts around the body. I'd get it around my chest and father treated me with calamine; there wasn't much else he could do to help me.

Filip went into overdrive when I was ill. He really shone at that time and, over the weeks, our grandparents got a little better and the room we lived in wasn't the hospital ward it had been. For me, it was a painful illness, but I didn't complain, how could I when we were all suffering so badly, everyday a battle to survive, a fight for your life. Eventually, I recovered, thinking it was, perhaps, a sign of better things to come.

The day my grandfather passed away was cold and miserable. I recall frost on the ground and a sharpness in the air. I came home with Filip after our morning rounds and my father stopped us in the doorway. "Your grandfather has passed on, he died in his sleep and was in no pain, he did not suffer," he said whilst holding in his emotions. We all held onto each other as if our legs had given way.

The weight of his death was a heavy burden. He'd been my friend as well as my grandfather and I adored him. I would miss his company for the rest of my life. My grandmother was distraught, she would cry for weeks afterwards. Followed by family and friends, we gave him a funeral as best we could, wrapped simply in a shroud. He passed away on 23rd February, 1941, a date that I couldn't forget easily as it was little Anna's birthday, one we didn't celebrate that year.

At that point in my life, my grandfather's passing was the hardest thing I'd have to go through and my brother and sister's pain was awful to observe. Little Anna suffered a lot, she missed her 'gaga' as she called him. Her tears hard to take on board, it compounded my own suffering.

It was at my grandfather's funeral that the SS showed themselves to be what they were, a portent of things to come.

The gunfire seemed to come from nowhere but the mourners fell to the ground like rag dolls. Blood spat out of people as they fell, life ebbing out of them. They ran as the gunfire burst through the air, rapid shots firing into the center of the crowd that had gathered for the burial.

There was no God in this world, he'd stopped keeping score and deserted us, there was no fairness in all of this, a regime that hated us for our religion and for who we were; cruelty was dished out daily. Children were treated the same as adults and were beaten and shot – we thought we were in hell but the reality was we were only at the front door.

A friend I'd gotten to know quite well, 'Ivan', was shot in the head at close range spraying blood over the SS officer's uniform, the one who'd killed him. His anger manifested itself upon the person he'd just executed and was terrifying. He kicked the corpse in a frenzied attack, simply because of the blood on his uniform; the world seemed to be run by psychopaths.

Ivan's death was cruel and vicious but at least it was quick, he didn't have time to suffer. In a strange way, I wished for an ending like that if I was to succumb to the brutality.

Twenty three people died that day, for no reason, a massacre with no justice at the end of it, simply the start of what was to come. The months that followed were a rapid decline in the survival of the people of the ghetto, starvation became an everyday thing, people died on the streets, their bodies lying lifeless like mannequins and children slept in the open, their parents clearly dead. Nobody was there to care for them though some did try their best, simply prolonging the truth; they were never going to make it through the winter. It was clear what was happening, systematically the nazis were starving us to death and blocking food coming in.

As a family, we still mourned our grandfather but we were suffering physically also, all of us malnourished as the lack of food spread through the ghetto. As hard as Filip and I tried there was just nothing we could do, the grip on the food chain had tightened and the Polish police were being vigorous in their pursuit of the smuggling.

Killings became everyday occurrences, the SS indiscriminately choosing people then marching them to their deaths, one bullet to the back of the head. They would play games, sick psychotic games, shooting every other person lined up for work duty. After one shooting twelve people lay dead in the road and twelve others, their lives spared, were simply ordered by an SS officer to "Get this shit off the road."

The life we'd had, though hard, no longer existed and death became your neighbour, one you kept away from as best you could but it seemed it would be just a matter of time before you couldn't avoid them any longer.

It was around this time they began to round people up from the street and march them to the railway station. Everyone was told they were going to labour camps. Men, women and children were taken, and I wondered why the children would go. How could they really contribute towards the Nazi cause? Maybe it was to keep families together I thought, how wrong we all were. The children, the little innocents, marched away with a prized toy in their arms unaware of what was to come; the horrors that would await them when they arrived. For the most part, we all were.

Oh, it's not that some of us hadn't heard the rumours. Most of the people we worked with on the black market were part of a newly formed resistance movement. They would tell of people who'd made it back from the east and spoke of camps where everyone from the trains were being gassed in buildings and then burnt in large pits. Although I asked them not to speak of this to Filip, I think he found out but we never discussed it between us. I suppose it was too dark to speak of.

As I'd never spoken to any of these 'escapees' myself, I found it difficult to believe but the more I saw the more I realised it was what most probably awaited us all.

I told the resistance people I was in the Policja and my brother was about to join when we were rounded up for the ghetto and they accepted us into the fold. We'd be of value to them I was told. They'd recognised our worth and had grown to trust us and we'd realised we couldn't just sit and accept the situation as fate.

Papa had supported us in our rebellious ways, he was ok with the smuggling, it brought benefits but he was against any violence and because of this, I told Filip not to mention the resistance. What they didn't know they didn't need to worry about.

On a cold night, we met with people from beyond the ghetto. A crude tunnel had been dug beneath the wall by the resistance which emerged in a block overlooking the Jewish sector. We were moving arms and some homemade explosives from the building when an alert was sounded. The SS had descended on the street. Panic set in, but Filip calmly collected everything in front of him, wrapped it in a large cloth he'd pulled from the wall and made for the cellar entrance to the tunnel. I had been dragged elsewhere and ended up leaving the building by a kitchen window, finding myself crouching in an alleyway with two others, watching the soldiers assault another block further along the street.

For an age, we remained in the cold, damp alley until someone found us and told us it was safe to return through the tunnel. I'd no idea what had happened to Filip or whether he'd made it back safely.

Emerging from the ghetto entrance, I made it to the street, hugging the building line as I tried to return home. I hesitated at the entrance to a courtyard, catching my breath and taking my bearings. A voice behind me softly called, "I'm here. It's me. Filip."

I turned and there he was in the shadows, still carrying the blanket and its contents. After the initial joy of finding him safe, I scolded him for still having the contraband. To be found with it or even near it was an immediate death sentence. We retreated to a nearby alley which was even darker where we stumbled upon a grid in the floor. It took a bit of effort but we managed to prise it open. It was one of the sewers and you could just about drop down into it.

A more perfect place to hide our burden we were not going to find in the circumstances so we stuffed everything into the murky waters within. Replacing the cover, we made our way towards home, keeping to the darkest shadows but it became obvious there was an alert on. The Ghetto Police were patrolling alongside the Polish 'Blue' Police and we were forced to sit in a secluded little courtyard affair until morning when we hoped to blend into the background as people woke and went about their day.

It had been so cold we held onto each other, using our body heat to stay warm. I didn't dare sleep and spent the next hours deep in thought and worry. Filip slept fitfully. It was hard to think my little brother had grown so fast in the ghetto. There was a maturity about him that came through. He was a born fighter, much more so than me. He seemed at his best in these turbulent times yet as I looked at him, exhausted in my arms, he was still only a boy.

The cold night brought sunshine in the morning that melted the slight frost and we waited until it was safe to merge with the general public. Walking down the street, we both felt a small battle had been won, but it was short-lived.

Back at the room, we received a grilling from Mama and Papa, both came down pretty hard on us but I took the brunt, being the eldest. I accepted it, you didn't argue with your parents, they had the experience we did not. I made up a story of innocence and bad timing, my brother nodded in agreement. I'm not sure Papa was fooled but he didn't explore the possibilities.

Filip was grounded, or shall I say he was told he was, the fact he ignored that ruling was proof of his maturity as a growing man or his defiance as a youth. He wasn't being disrespectful to our parents, he realised what we were doing was more important and he saw the bigger picture.

He would develop without my input and go off and do his own thing, often also bringing back food for the family which was essential and much appreciated. He was very good at being a scrounger and found ways that I couldn't. He *made* things happen.

An intelligent boy, I was very proud of him as were the rest of the family, he'd accepted the ghetto and adapted to it. Whilst they didn't like what he was doing and feared for him, my parents still admired the boy they had brought up.

Although we tried hard it never seemed enough and I'd noticed Filip and little Anna had lost more weight, I could see it clearly, my parents also. It was disturbing to see your family looking gaunt with lack of food, the developing deep-set eyes being the obvious sign of malnourishment.

Soon, my grandmother refused to eat. She would say it was more important for us children to survive. Her sacrifice was a choice she made. In her methodology, we had a life ahead of us and she had lived hers, this is how desperate our situation was. Our mother accepted her decision which couldn't have been an easy choice but 'Babcia' could be quite forceful when needed. It was the reality of our situation. It was awful to eat your grandmother's food but you did as you were told, as hard as it was.

She died two months to the day after our grandfather and it was dreadful, the reality setting in about how short-lived a person's life could be in the ghetto. The manipulation of the food supply by the SS was killing people in droves. Their plan was working, we were dying without their direct input and although they murdered at will, the majority of deaths were through starvation. Little Anna was distraught and inconsolable. Her nana was her friend more than any of us and she played with her all the time. She was beside herself with grief and to see that was truly heartbreaking.

Then came the clearances. Dragged out of the blocks opposite, families were forced to stand in the middle of the cold street by groups of soldiers. Everyone was brought out, the frail, elderly and children. Those who attempted to run were shot.

Pulled from the crowd, seemingly for no reason, men and women were told to form a line against a wall, hands on their heads. An SS officer walked down the line firing a single shot from his Luger into the head of a victim, the next in line waiting patiently for their turn. All fifteen were shot dead, the officer pausing only to change his magazine after he shot his eighth victim, cold and calculated as could be.

The surviving throng were marched off towards the train station. Filip, Tomasz and I watched, standing back from the window so as not to be seen, hands held tightly across our mouths to stifle any involuntary noise. The others gathered at the far side of the room, trying to distract themselves and Anna.

Later that night, the soldiers returned, searching with dogs for those who had hidden away. It was a difficult night for us to bear.

The actions continued in adjoining streets and then further afield. It paid dividends to have good connections with the Judenrat, the Jewish governing council, and it seems that was my father's contribution to our survival, besides the pittance he was able to make from his work as a pharmacist dispensing the medicines the council and the black market were able to provide.

In the night, with their torches, dogs and searchlights, the SS stormed our block. As if fear of the bullet wasn't enough, they used the dogs for maximum intimidation. Five soldiers burst into our room shouting, "Kommen sie mit! Kommen sie mit!' followed repeatedly with "Raus! Raus!" as we hurriedly did as we were told. Father called, "Do as they say, do not falter." Mama was screaming and little Anna had begun to cry from sheer terror. I knew Filip wanted to fight back but I gripped his arm tightly and told him firmly, "No Filip, do as we're told, survival is all that matters. This isn't the time."

In the courtyard, we lined up and stood quietly as an SS officer walked up and down awaiting the rest of the block, impatiently shouting "Beeilung!" (hurry up) to the passing soldiers. Two officers on horseback watched over the proceedings as though judging how the SS officers performed.

I looked around, Tomasz and Kinga were missing. In the chaos of the situation, we'd not noticed they hadn't immediately followed us out and for a moment I wished them well, somehow they'd escaped from this mayhem.

But then, a commotion at the block entrance and they were running towards the lineup followed by a soldier who was shouting angrily. They pushed their way into the crowd but the officer grabbed Tomasz and dragged him back out. We all knew what was going to happen. The officer drew his pistol as Kinga dashed to join her husband. Standing next to him, she held his hand. In a split second, they'd collapsed to the ground, blood flowing from their heads like water from an annoyingly stiff tap you're struggling to turn off.

I felt little Anna's legs go and I just managed to sweep her up before she fell. She'd wet herself. She shouldn't have seen such a thing, they'd murdered Tomasz and Kinga in front of us. She was shaking, yet she knew instinctively not to cry out. I held her close, trying to comfort her as her entire body trembled. My father hugged my mother tightly and Filip just stood and stared defiantly.

Orders were given to march us through the ghetto. It was bitterly cold and we had no coats or warm clothing but we did as we were told. Through the streets, we saw others in the ghetto watch on, probably wondering when it would be their turn.

We spent the next hours shivering on the railway station platform. Although many had coats and luggage, the people from our block had only what they stood in. When the train arrived, the dogs strained their leashes snapping at everyone within range and we were herded into the bare, soulless railway boxcars.

We didn't know where we were going or how long the journey would be but I had an awful, dark gut sickening feeling that I was perhaps the only one who really knew. Papa held on to Anna, she was in deep shock, the sort that makes you ill, I could see it. Her body was stiff, she was catatonic. It was all too much for her and something I'd never forget was her little face. It still haunts me. In another time, I would have prayed but I knew, now, it was pointless.

It's difficult to describe the conditions in those boxcars. There were no facilities and people urinated, or worse, where they stood. We stopped for a long while in some sidings after an hour or so and

I managed to push my way to the exit door and catch a glimpse of the name of the stop. It was Opoczno. I knew of this place and knew it was on the main route from Warsaw to Krakow.

Near the walls of the carriage, there was air but it was cold. The further to the center you managed to get it began to get warmer but the air was not so fresh. People passed out and people died. It was hard to tell the dead apart from the living because they remained wedged upright. As the journey continued, we organised ourselves and started a sort of rota system as best we could, moving people back and forth from the cold to the warmth and back again. The dead sometimes fell to the floor and all we could do was to stand on them. Eventually, we slowly pulled into a station and stopped. The sign said 'Oswiecim'. The doors slid back and guards began to shout "Raus! Raus!" We stumbled from the carriage and Mama took Anna's hand. Almost immediately, an SS officer walked the line repeatedly calling in both Polish and German, "There is nothing to worry about. The men are going to the work camp and the others are just going to the family camp not far away. You will all see each other soon."

We men were pushed and cattled to one end of the platform, snarling dogs filling the void between us and the women and children. Men in blue striped pajamas helped the sick and elderly to one side. Several open-backed trucks waited nearby whilst bodies were pulled unceremoniously out and onto the ground.

Standing in the line, I was momentarily relieved to catch sight of Mama with her arms around Anna, comforting her. I waved wildly at her, calling to Filip and Papa. She'd seen us and both waved back before the column was marched away. As they left, I heard one of the female guards shouting, "It is only two kilometres then you shall have showers and some bread and hot coffee."

Suddenly, a struggle broke out in our line, a man separated from his wife fought to stay with her. They simply shot him. The SS officer walked amongst our group saying, "They are being taken for delousing and for the showers. There is nothing to worry about." He smiled as he said, "Women and children first." We marched off in the opposite direction for our first introduction to the gates and 'Arbeit Macht Frei'.

Brick barracks surrounded us. It looked like an old military camp. Guards with clipboards were asking questions. "I am a carpenter," I heard someone say and he was sent to join a line that faced several tables at which soldiers sat. Another said, 'Professor' and was sent to join the other group.

I looked quickly back and forth, some men with white coats and stethoscopes walked up and down behind the tables occasionally pointing at someone or other. The group the professor joined were predominantly older men, 50 and over, there were no tables and no white coats. I told Filip and Papa, "We are carpenters. Tell them you are a carpenter." Papa tried to protest but I gripped his arm tightly and said, "For pity's sake, Papa, you are a carpenter now!" I saw the dawning of realisation in his eyes.

We all made it through the selection and with

others were taken for what they called 'disinfection'. Made to strip in the open and leave any other possessions, we were hosed down before being given the blue striped 'pajamas' and ill-fitting wooden shoes. We had our heads shaved and received our tattoos.

We didn't know at that time we'd never see Mama and Anna again. I should have realised, given what I'd been told, but hope can be a terrible thing, it makes you cling to a lie until, exhausted, it leaves you like a thief in the night.

In days to come, unable to take the burden, the others when asked would pass us off by saying they would be in the women's camp and everything was fine but eventually we became 'wiser'. We learned the truth about the disinfection blocks in the woods at Birkenau.

That night Papa wept, he must have suspected even then. Filip and I prayed with all our hearts that the innocence of our sister would save her and that Mama would look after her. We knew Mama wouldn't ever let her go because she was strong and she would fight for her with a love that had no beginning or end. She adored her baby girl and would protect her no matter what. We convinced ourselves they would be ok, we'd just be separated for a short time and then be reunited as a family; our perfect family, as if we were somehow different. But Mama and Anna were taken to the woods, told to undress and then murdered in 'the little red house', their bodies dragged to the pits beyond and burnt.

"Just a child and so beautiful. Surely they would see that?" "Surely, yes, surely they'd see she's just a child."

Chapter 3

Lukas Baur

January 1994

Luiza sat down looking worried. "What is it, are you ill?" she said.

"No, I'm fine, Luiza. I've something to tell you about my past, the war to be precise." I then spent several minutes talking as gently as I could explaining to a woman I'd been married to for nearly forty years that I had kept a secret from her and I'd been a prisoner in Auschwitz.

"You didn't tell me, all these years, Emil. All this time, and you didn't tell me!" She sat there confused. "Krakow, we went there," she said, attempting to work it out. "This was the reason?"

"Yes, Luiza. I'm sorry. I'm so sorry you have to go through this, it's not my intention to hurt you." I explained. "I just wanted to put it behind me. It was the worst time of my life and I didn't want it to be any part of ours. We've had a good one, haven't we?"

"Of course we have," she replied, soothingly. "But you should have told me, Emil."

"I couldn't. I blanked it out as if it didn't happen, as though it was a story I'd heard told by somebody else, that's how I dealt with it, put it in a box and stuff it in a cupboard, it was the only way," I explained. "I had a family, Luiza. Mother, father, brother and sister." I wept as I thought of them, lips pursed upwards to form a strong jaw to stop the pain from taking over.

"Will you tell me what happened?" she asked.

"No, I can't, it's still in the box. I'm only telling you now because there is something I have to do," I replied.

"What do you have to do? What is it that after forty years you have to tell me your secret to be able to do this thing? What is it Emil?" she pleaded, clearly in shock.

How was I to tell her what had happened to me? How would I explain Aleksy Markowski and what he'd given me to do? I tried over the next half hour and told her Aleksy was ill, very ill and he'd handed me documents that needed further research to catch war criminals.

Again she pleaded. "Why you and why now and what was it they did that was so bad?"

"Luiza, your mind couldn't imagine the crimes these men took part in. I don't want to explain them to you, they are too awful to speak of but trust me, they need arresting and brought before the courts, they're criminals."

"I can't take this in, you're seventy-three years of age and you're hunting down war criminals? It doesn't make sense at all. Yesterday you were a pensioner enjoying your retirement from the force and today you're Simon Wiesenthal hunting war criminals! This is a nightmare, Emil. You can't do this to your family," she pronounced. I started to speak but stalled and gathered my thoughts. "Luiza, have I always been a good man and looked after my family? I've worked and done things in my life that others wouldn't have. You know, I've seen things that would turn your stomach and you know full well

I've done all of those things to give us and the children a good life," I said.

"Yes, Emil, I'm not doubting what you've done. You're a good man, the very best but this is just too much," she countered.

I took her hands in mine. "I've never asked you for anything, never needed anything more than your love and I'm now asking you to support me because this is something I have to do, this is my purification, Luiza. Auschwitz broke me, it gave me demons I've kept secret all my life. I've seen things nobody should ever see. I can never explain Auschwitz to you. It was unthinkable but here," I showed her my arm and the scar where my number was tattooed, the scar I'd told her years ago was just a burn. "This is who I am. To the Nazis, I was a number, my life was worthless." I broke down. "Just a number."

She wrapped her arms around me. "Come, Emil, don't cry," she told me as the tears flowed down her cheeks. "I love you, Emil Janowitz. You're my best friend. Whatever you do, I will support you. I wish what you were telling me wasn't so but it is and I'll support you," she said. We wiped our eyes and kissed each other softly. "I'll make us a nice hot drink," she smiled.

The file lay on the table in the living room. I picked it up, flicking to a page where Lukas Baur's picture greeted me. I immediately recognised his Auschwitz photo and realised I wouldn't need to revisit the place again to see the wall. Markowski had all the photographs we needed.

Baur's face was clear, the photo in good condition and what hit me was all the things he'd done; as soon as I saw his photograph it was like instant recall. Names connect people but photographs identify a person's deeds and I knew this was the man I'd witnessed commit murder. He'd done so much in his short time in the camp. As an Austrian block leader, he'd affiliated with the SS and spoke German; another advantage over the prisoners. I wondered if it had been a condition of him becoming a Kapo.

As I read the file, it explained how he'd entered Auschwitz, one of 23,000 Austrian and German

Jews. He'd arrived from the "Theresienstadt" ghetto camp in Bohemia and been made a Kapo shortly after arrival.

He was a big man, at entry weighing 200lbs which coming from a ghetto was odd, also a possible reason for being chosen as a block leader. It then went into detail about the crimes he committed whilst in charge of prisoners; the beating to death of a man was highlighted by the words 'Witness Ezra Farber Page 27' whilst assisting the SS in the gassing process of thousands of Jews was highlighted with 'Witness Ezra Farber Page 29'. Then there was the hanging of the twelve Latvian Jews. In total, the next few pages listed forty-two crimes, any one of which you'd hang for. My head spun, so I joined Luiza in the kitchen. She gave me a coffee and I gave her a smile.

File still at hand, I returned to the living room to read through the pages that detailed more crimes, most of which I wasn't aware of. Markowski must have interviewed many prisoners over the years, some of the statements must have been 30 years old.

To have so many witnesses for the crimes and all this information was phenomenal and showed why it had taken so long to compile.

"Aleksander Bichler Page 33" was one witness. "Maharam Deichman Page 17" another. On it went, all witnessed and documented. As I flicked forward in the file, I found signed and dated written statements. First-hand witness evidence of the crimes Lukas Baur committed whilst a Kapo.

I flipped the pages back and there was a photo of him taken possibly in the 1980s. He'd aged a lot but still had that cold-hearted mean look on his face. He'd changed his name! Josef Weber. It jumped out of the page at me. Escaping the Russians by the skin of his teeth, he'd headed to Munich, changed his name to Weber, a common name of the time, and simply blended in.

A butcher by trade, which didn't surprise me, he'd worked firstly on the market then, later, bought a shop in the side streets, living locally not far away. He'd opened a bar, in 1983, allowing his son and daughter to run it whilst he continued with the butcher's shop. There was an address and the information he'd retired in 1985 leaving his son to run the business.

He liked to frequent the bar his daughter ran *and* his wife, it said, was still alive but no more was given. The man had lived a normal existence, reinventing himself as though all the crimes had been somebody else's. He'd be 78 years of age by now. Would he recognise me if I walked into the bar? I questioned that. I had changed also, not so gaunt now. I wore eyeglasses most of the time and made a note to do so before meeting Baur, or Josef Weber as he was now known.

Luiza was weeping in the kitchen when I returned to top up my coffee cup. I tried to comfort her but nothing would stop her tears and I felt I'd let her down. All I could do was apologise. I didn't have a choice in this, it was something I needed to do for myself, to heal the pain, and I needed to do it for those who couldn't.

I told her, "You know, my brother was a wonderful boy. He looked after us all in the ghetto. I was very proud of him and my sister was a sweet child. She didn't deserve to be born in those times. I cannot explain it, Luiza, but my pain overwhelms me and I'm forced to do this. I have to be able to look myself in the eyes and know I did all I could, all any man could do in such circumstances."

"I know, Emil. I'm not crying for myself. I cry for you, for your pain, for your losses and all you have gone through. I wish I'd known, I would have helped you, I would have loved you more," she said and we both held onto each other tightly, like life itself depended on it.

"You couldn't love me more. It isn't possible. You've been a good wife." Then, attempting to lighten the mood and looking deep into her eyes, "I've taught you well. It's far too late to try and train up a new one now."

"You, mister, won't be getting any supper tonight," she said looking at me, nodding her head wisely, then wiping her eyes with a tissue.

"I'm sorry. It's a surprise as much to me as it is to you. I thought I'd forgotten about all of this but now, I know it won't go away unless I make it," I said.

The next day, I walked to Greenwich with Luiza. We'd plan this together but I insisted I'd travel alone. The travel agent was called Cruise and Travel Inc, off the East Putnam Road. It was one I'd used before and I knew the woman I was talking to, although I'd forgotten her name. Luckily, she had a badge. Karen was a large lady, with long dark hair and a pretty face. I enquired about tickets for Munich in March.

"Oh! The beer festival, you want to take in the Oktoberfest," she stated.

"No, not really," I replied, cautiously deciding to say nothing. "It'll be a cultural tour, maybe a three-day trip. That should do it." She tapped away on her computer and after what seemed an eternity she came back with, "Thursday to Sunday, March 18th to the 21st. Will that accommodate your timings?"

"Perfect," I agreed and went on to pay for my flights and accommodation near the center. I'd made the booking and committed to the job.

Luiza looked at me and said, "You're really going to do this aren't you." "I have to. It's bigger than me. I'm just Emil Janowitz, a small man from Luborzyca. Life has been very good to me in some respects but the head's side of this coin has to be dealt with so I can grab the tail's side and get on with my life." I put the ticket in my breast pocket, thanked Karen for her help then took Luiza for some lunch at L'Escale, a French Restaurant in the Delamar Hotel, overlooking the waterside and known for its good food.

We dined and tried to speak of what was to come but I was at a loss to tell her, the reality being I was going into this blind. All I knew was I'd go to the bar and try to identify Josef Weber as he was now known. I'd already done a little research and discovered it was called 'Augustiner-Keller'.

I'd found it in the central library on Lambarde Square. They had several computers in there connected to the internet and Ellie, one of their assistants, helped me and printed off the details.

I had a name and the address of where Lukas Baur spent his time drinking. Before I'd go, I made sure I was fully up to date on the file I'd been left with, it would take me some time but I had nothing else that urgently needed my attention before Munich.

I needed to know everything about him, most importantly, if he appeared in police records since the war. That was something I hoped to be able to call in favours for. I found myself falling into my old Police routines which would be helpful. Over a forty year police career, I'd seen most things, from murders to suicide. You name it, I'd done it but I'd thought all of that was in my past along with Auschwitz.

Over the next week, I studied the file in detail. There were over five hundred pieces of paper in there and he'd been extensively scrutinised including little things like the schools his now adult children attended to his insurance details. He'd been watched from afar and had no idea someone was detailing his life.

Aleksy Markowski had used public records to find Lukas Baur and uncover his new identity, address, telephone number and new social security number. He'd found Baur's credibility as a business owner was dubious. He'd nothing in his name, the last one was seemingly owned by his wife and, whilst working at the market, he'd found himself a business associate in Max Friedrich who had a shop in a prime position, although he was struggling to realise its potential. Friedrich, of course, became the senior partner and the tax returns were in his name. Separating the businesses in 1985, Weber had kept the butchers and the tax return that year had shown it as a tax loss. His partner, Friedrich, had disappeared and a check on him showed he'd simply vanished, no forwarding address and no name change. Essentially, the tax loss was accepted but Friedrich's tax return the next year was not filed.

This all looked suspicious to me, a missing person who'd been in a partnership with Weber and allegedly, according to the tax return, paid off for his share of the business with 120,000 Deutche Marks, a significant amount of money – the equivalent to about $65,000 at the time. It didn't feel right. I already knew the character of the man, there was no doubt he was a killer but it was just something in the file that Aleksy had put in, albeit not in sequence, so he may not have come to the same conclusion I had.

My flight left at 1830 Eastern Standard Time and was scheduled to get me in around 0725. With the time difference, it would make the flight eight hours. Luiza came to the airport with me. She'd told the kids I'd been called back into the police on a historical case.They were shocked but they believed the lie.

It was a necessary little white one simply to save us from the fact that my daughter was like a dog with a bone if she felt she was being left out of the loop; she'd just hound you until you found it easier telling her. Luckily, Luiza had chosen the day of my departure to tell them both and it hadn't given them much time to question me.

Meanwhile, I went out and bought the mobile phone that Aleksy had told me to. Having given mine up when I left the force, I didn't feel the need for one, a peaceful life was what I'd planned, how wrong I'd been on that.

I chose a Nokia 1011, it served its purpose, a big grey brick yet smaller than the one I'd had in the force and it kept its charge for a long time. I put our home number on it and the mobile phone number Aleksy had left me in the file and that was it – I didn't want to encourage any phone calls from Daniel and especially not Lena, I'd deal with them when I returned.

The flight went well, I arrived at Munich International Airport at 0715 and by the time I'd gotten through customs it was more like 0830. I jumped in a taxi, a cream Mercedes C Class, and headed for the Alpen Hotel which was a short walk from the center and importantly only a fifteen minute walk from the Augustiner-Keller bar where my target would be. I phoned Luiza and told her I'd arrived safe.

I planned to settle into the hotel and then pay a visit in the evening, testing the field. The fact I was in the same vicinity as the Kapo from my past who'd butchered and colluded with the Nazis filled me with excitement. I would be his return to Auschwitz.

The walk to the bar took me past the Kindermuseum and then right, following the tram line. I probably could have jumped on one but it was only a fifteen minute walk and I figured the exercise would do me good. A right turn just after the "Commerzbank," and, at the bottom of the road, I found the bar.

It was a large place which surprised me. I walked in and had a look around, it was well kept and laid out to serve food. I glanced through a menu: Bavarian and International cuisine. It had a substantive outdoor area but I stayed inside, ordered an Augustiner Weissbier and took a seat. The wheat beer tasted refreshing; I hadn't realised I needed it so much. The décor was mainly wooden and, all in all, it was a very traditional Austrian bar. I ordered a German sausage skillet with potatoes and sauerkraut and settled for the night.

People were coming in and having a beer and a chat after work, some still wearing their workwear. Mainly, they spoke German but now and then I discerned someone speaking with the Austrian dialect which I recognised from my earlier life.

I listened in on the conversations and it seemed Bayern Munich were leading the Bundesliga. Werder Bremen, the defending champions, were faltering but Eintracht Frankfurt were looking dangerous because of 'Tony Yeboah', a player of some considerable skill by all accounts.

The bar staff changed at 8pm and a woman in her early forties took over. I was transfixed, was she the daughter of Josef Weber? I decided to stay until ten. Around 9pm a man appeared, striped jumper, jacket and chinos with brown shoes, his hair was thin on top.

He took off the jacket and placed it on the back of a stool, ordered the same sort of beer I had and spoke to the woman behind the bar in a stern manner. He was asking questions about the bar; had the delivery arrived? How much had they taken that day? From his manner, he was annoyed but that was how Lukas Baur had always looked. It was him.

All these years had passed by and he was still alive, his eyes penetrating like he was analysing you. His nose had been broken at some stage, I noted. I didn't recall him having the injury in Auschwitz so assumed he must have picked on the wrong person at some point. He joined a group of men who were obviously regulars and they talked of football, mostly.

I couldn't believe I was sat in a bar in Munich with Lukas Baur, or Josef Weber as he was known. The temptation to shout over to him "Lukas Baur, you're identified," was almost overwhelming but I resisted and decided I'd just finish my beer and phone Aleksy to let him know I'd found him.

It seemed so easy but Aleksy had done all the hard work by trolling through the records and I knew how difficult and time consuming linking everything together would have been. I'd spent years on a case that eventually came to court and my evidence was crucial in putting the child killer, Ivo Fletcher, behind bars for murder.

I settled my tab with Josef Weber's daughter, left a tip and was just about to leave when he came over to me. My heart was pounding.

"You enjoyed the sausages, please come again," he said, with a smile. He hadn't recognised me.

"Yes, I did and I'll be back tomorrow," I informed him, my nerves holding strong. He gestured to his daughter to come over and clear the table and, as I turned, he grabbed my shoulder and threw his hand in mine. "Thank you for your custom, sir," he said, something he'd probably done a million times to each customer that passed his scrutiny.

As I left, I had an uneasy feeling. Lukas Baur was a clever man and I questioned my own thoughts. Had he actually recognised me and made a point of grabbing my hand to show his confidence or was I overthinking?

The day had gone well. I rang Luiza, letting her know I'd eaten and my room was comfortable. She told me she missed me and that the children had given her hell over me going away; Dad's retired. Why on earth would he come out of retirement? It didn't make sense, they'd insisted. I told her I'd sort it when I returned but it was a conversation I wasn't looking forward to having.

I then phoned Aleksy. He picked up immediately, one ring tone and he greeted me with, "Hello, have you identified him?"

I replied, "Yes, it's him but I'll spend a few more days whilst I'm here getting visuals to ensure I'm 100% correct in my memory. I'm here for another two nights anyway. I wasn't expecting to see him on the first night but believe me it is him," I reassured.

"Whatever you do now, do not blow it, do not give yourself away and do not expose him. You've done your job identifying him, only go back to verify your target, you've done well," he said. I was surprised at the praise, concise as it was. Aleksy Markowski didn't come across as someone who would give any at all. I took the accolade and said I'd call again.

I'd make my notes up when I returned to my room. Yes, I thought, it had been a very good day. I was pleased with myself for not losing it, I'd been professional, even though my hatred for Lukas Baur was eating into me. To catch him and punish him in the courts, I'd have to play the game.

I had a brandy coffee in the hotel bar before I went to bed, a demon had been exorcised and that night I fell asleep easily, content I'd done a good days work.

The door burst open and Lukas Baur came at me, in his hand was a wooden baton. The first blow caught me on the right arm, the pain was intense. "I'll fucking kill you," he shouted whilst smashing the club against my body, blow after blow. One caught me on the side of my mouth and the blood poured, I could taste it. I was in real trouble. I was struggling to get to my feet to defend myself.

"You come after me, after all these years? I'll fucking kill you, you fucking pig," he hissed and the blows kept coming. For someone so old he was strong, he'd lost nothing of his nature, he was still a killer, an unashamed brutal animal. Somehow, I managed to stand up and tried to fend off the blows but it was futile, he had the advantage of the club and he was furious. I felt the blood trickling down my neck, it was warm and thick and I realised I would die if I didn't do something. I grabbed a vase from a table and, with strength I didn't know I had, smashed it into his face cutting my own hand in doing so.

He grunted and staggered back but came straight back at me. "Jesus!" I cried out. How could he be so strong at his age. He struck another blow and this time it broke my arm. I felt physically sick but could only think, "Shit! Luiza will be devastated." How had I got myself in this mess, how had he known, he must have followed me back to the hotel after I'd left the bar.

Suddenly, he pulled out a gun and I stood still, my arm a mess. He levelled it in one hand pointing at me with the other. "Fucking Polish Jew, you should have died in Auschwitz." He pointed the gun towards my head and I stood frozen, waiting for the bullet.

"You're going to die now," he said. I heard the bang, bang, bang and woke.

"Good morning, sir, this is your wake up call." The words hit as I leapt out of bed. "Oh Jesus! It was a dream," I said out loud, gasping for breath. "Thank you!" I called, "Thank you, very much." A muffled reply of "You're welcome." Then silence.

I was covered in sweat, even in my dreams it hunted me, so real and vivid. I'd had them before, mainly about beatings in Auschwitz and Luiza had witnessed them but I'd lied to her for years about the cause.

I showered, the dream still fresh in my mind, and felt my arm which was oddly tender just where he'd hit me in my dream.

I tried to put it out of my mind but it was disturbing. I'd believed it was happening to me. It was almost more of a shock to wake up, it was so real.

The remainder of the weekend, I spent time in the bar. I'd speak several times to Yvette, Baur's daughter. She confirmed the connection. She seemed a pleasant girl and spoke of her father. "He's a bully, he shouts at me all the time. I do everything and it is never enough." I got the impression she was afraid of him and may have witnessed his anger at some point yet I also got the feeling she still loved him; he was her father after all.

Her brother Hugo showed up on the Saturday night, introduced himself and thanked me for the custom, seemingly it was a family trait.

I kept clear of 'Josef Weber', I didn't want to raise suspicion. I'd see him one more time on my trip, the Saturday night, he again came in late and said hello, recognising me from the Thursday. He went about his business and didn't trouble me.

In all honesty, his children seemed decent people and I did think *what am I doing here?* It was fifty years since Auschwitz, but I soon forgot that when he had to throw a drunk out. "Hugo, just get him out," he shouted as the man fell against the bar, smashing a glass. Hugo was acting really professionally, attempting to encourage the man out politely, when Baur pushed past him and started shoving the drunk out. "Raus!" he shouted "Raus!" his anger clear, "Raus aus meiner Bar! Du bist betrunken!" He manhandled the man roughly and forcefully threw him out onto the sidewalk whilst Hugo watched shaking his head, clearly disturbed by the change in the atmosphere his father had created.

You could tell by his mannerisms, Baur had no connection with people, he would have beaten the man if he had the chance – just someone who'd had one drink too many, an innocent man who'd apologised for breaking the glass. He'd made a mistake and Baur jumped on it with no sympathy or understanding for the situation, he just wanted him out and didn't care how he achieved it. I realised then he had no empathy, a probable narcissist, his actions certainly didn't fit in with the people around him and I wondered if that was what caused him to be such a monster in Auschwitz.

A condition he may have been born with had caused such traits that came out under pressure but I stopped thinking and told myself "This is Lukas Baur, don't make excuses for him, he doesn't deserve it."

My visit had been successful overall, I'd found him and made a positive identification which had been confirmed by the family documented in his file. He'd shown his true colours on Saturday and I'd witnessed it, the man was still the same, the years hadn't mellowed him, he was still a nasty piece of work. I'd fulfilled my first job on the list.

Chapter 4
Jarmil Pleva

It was January 1944 and my father lined up for a work detail. Filip and I were to be taken separately to work in the factory at Auschwitz 3 – Monowitz. The winter had set in and snow filled the camp.

He was ill, his body was being eaten away by malnutrition, Filip's too but youth was on his side. I watched over the weeks as Papa's muscle mass wasted away.

His eyesight was the first to suffer; without his glasses, which were taken from him at registration, he was walking blind.

Starvation was wreaking havoc on everyone and the cold was worsening the overall conditions. He'd been smashed in the face by a guard which left a cut around his mouth that had become infected because of his poor health. It was heartbreaking to see.

He'd also been suffering from dysentery and, combined with a poor diet and the cold, he failed the selection. Standing some distance away, Filip and I were powerless to help him and the last we saw of him was as he was dragged away and placed on a cart with the other sick people. He didn't cry out or resist. The cart was pulled away by a group of prisoners.

We prayed he was going to the infirmary, that's what they always told us, but we feared the worst. Nature had taken a hold of his body and it became inevitable he'd succumb to a life threatening illness. In Auschwitz there was only one 'cure all' for such a thing. I suppose we knew, really, but simply didn't want to face the awful truth, preferring to delude ourselves that somehow, for us, it would be different. The delusion helped to assuage the guilt of having done nothing. There'd be no funeral, no words said, he was just gone and that was that.

Before that day, his eyes had been deep set with starvation. It disguised the good looks he'd been known for, our mother had told us he was a handsome young man when she'd met him.

He was a good man who gave much more than he took from life. Even in illness, he instilled into us both the need to survive and he, more than anyone, gave Filip and I our spirit. "Tell your story to the world, don't give up hope," he'd tell us both.

He'd clung to the belief our mother and sister had somehow survived the gas chamber and it had kept him going but I think he came to realise the futility of such a hope and the will to fight the infections slowly drained from him. He'd always done his best to shield us all from the realities.

We both struggled to come to terms with his death, once we'd admitted to ourselves he wasn't coming back. The loss of Papa was dreadful, a knife in our hearts. More than a father, he'd also been our friend.

Although we'd become used to death around us, it wasn't the same as this. We didn't know the others who'd died and we carried this malignant tumour around with us, deep inside, fearing for our own survival and fighting the guilt of daring to survive without him.

Filip was now 20 years of age, in my eyes still a boy, but he'd become hardened by the ghetto in

Warsaw and now Auschwitz. He'd mourned losing his father but held in as much as he could, not wanting to show the Kapo, Jarmil Pleva, any weakness.

Because of Filip's feisty spirit, Pleva had taken a dislike to my brother; they'd argued on a work detail and Pleva struck him. I picked my brother up from the mud and warned him he had to be careful, we only had each other and we had a duty to do as our father had told us – to survive.

Filip, was quiet, not knowing what to say but then turned to me and said, "We're going to die in here aren't we?" I grabbed his shoulders and told him, "No, Filip, we're going to get through all of this, we are stronger, we will survive." I hugged him tightly and he began to weep, I could feel him sobbing. It was then that I realised he was still just a boy inside. He'd been forced to grow up so quickly, no time to take it all in; losing his father had hit him hard and at this moment he was simply broken.

The young boy I held in my arms consoling had been so strong up until now and I was so proud of him. It was only natural for a young man to weep for his father but he'd been terrified for the first time, probably the same way as our little sister had been entering the gas chambers.

We'd both lived our lives to impress our parents, we'd never wanted to let them down and I was determined that we still wouldn't.

Our spirits were low over the next few weeks and Jarmil Pleva had noticed. He started picking his way into Filip's soul like the coward he was. He toyed with him, trying to provoke him knowing he had enough spirit to react, and knowing the SS would back a Kapo if Filip stepped out of line.

I warned him of this and told him he must never retaliate, even though we both knew what kind of rat Pleva was. I'd remind him whenever the Kapo came looking for trouble, "You have to just take it Filip, remember what Papa said."

I knew my brother was hot headed and still full of anger for what had happened to his father. Pleva realised it too and struck him with his baton on every occasion he could.

He enjoyed picking on the weak in the block, the ones who couldn't fight back, knowing he had the protection of the SS. He thought he was safe, immune, but he'd find out he was not.

One day, the women appeared through the barbed wire, on the other side of the fence. Because of the length of absence from a loved one, the camp went into a frenzy. Alsatians tethered to SS guards chased them, stretching their leashes to attack. There was screaming and confusion from the female side, worry and stress from the men's.

I was looking in hope for a glance of my mother and little Anna but there was nothing. It was a hope we still clung to, like our father.

The women were run into a distant block, disappearing down the ramp and we were dispersed. We never saw them again.

I stood looking back at the building they ran screaming towards and later the smoke would gush from the chimney spreading ash across the camp like snowfall. I think it was then that I realised hope was a wasted 'emotion'.

I gave Filip as much as I could of my rations as Pleva was withholding some of his simply to spite him. He'd try to refuse but I countered his resistance by telling him I'd managed to scavenge something earlier on. Sometimes it was true, finding oneself on a work detail near any kitchen facility opportunities could not be missed. I'd eat whatever scraps I found and eat them immediately. If I was caught carrying or hiding them I'd get a bullet to the head.

He was spirited though and he'd take whatever Jarmil Pleva would throw at him even though he was clearly suffering, his eyes deep set and haunted. He was ten times the man Pleva would ever be.

I knew I'd have to protect my brother from Pleva as best I could, the man had taken a dislike to him and, drawn like a moth to a flame, he became a danger to Filip's life. He wouldn't let my brother escape his grasp, it was clear he wanted him dead and I couldn't allow that to happen.

He'd follow him about the camp just waiting for an opportunity to pounce upon him with the baton, each blow taking its toll on Filip who became weaker over time. A typical bully looking for weakness and taking advantage, he had to be stopped.

The decision to kill him came quite easily to me, it was either my brother or him and that just wasn't a choice; I couldn't let him destroy my brother. I'd pick my moment somewhere away from the guards.

I didn't tell Filip because he'd likely attempt to do it himself to protect me. I told no one, it would have been too much of a risk; I didn't know who was in Pleva's circle. I'd learnt very early on to trust nobody, to keep my mouth shut. If you were going to kill someone, do it on your own, quietly.

Days passed and I watched from the sidelines as he tormented my brother and beat him. I did nothing but be ready if he went too far. I thought *my time will come*, he'd make that crucial mistake at some point. I was taking in the anger, absorbing it and making it a strength to destroy him with.

Filip was by now very weak and I worried for him, his bones protruding from his emaciated body, his face gaunt and I could see the fear in his eyes.

Although my own health was suffering, my thoughts were for my brother, I knew he couldn't take another beating, I had to act soon. It was not long before the opportunity presented itself.

I saw Pleva walking to a newly constructed quarantine hut, the prisoners building it also had to use it as accommodation. He entered the block house from the end that was viewable from several guard towers. I saw him do it and decided to enter from the opposite end which was only visible from one tower in the distance.

I'd watched the prisoner detail marched off earlier so was fairly sure Pleva would be alone there. If he wasn't, I'd make it up as I went along, lure him away with a non-existent urgent message from an SS man and kill him at the first opportunity en route. It was time for action, not fear.

The Kapo on my work detail was one of the very few who still had some decency. He looked at me, it was as if he knew something, then he turned away, shielding his eyes, studying something in the distance. I was gone, taking my shovel with me.

Having waited briefly until the guard in the tower was looking elsewhere, I entered the block. Pleva was writing on a clipboard, his baton under his arm. I said I had a message for him, placed my shovel on the floor and stood to attention, allaying any of his suspicions. Then, I told him an SS Officer had instructed him to report to the Judenrampe immediately.

He ordered me to return to the Officer to tell him he was on his way. I bent down to recover my shovel, stood up quickly with it in a full swing and smashed it across his head. I used all of my power and his skull split like a coconut. I didn't aim for anything else, I did it to stop any calls for help and had wanted to stun him enough so I could tell him why he would die but I'd hit him that hard I killed him instantly. My only regret was he hadn't suffered the way he'd made my brother suffer.

He'd fallen alongside the communal latrine that almost ran the length of the hut. I quickly removed several covers and 'poured' Pleva's body into the liquid shit below. I threw in the clipboard, pen and baton for good measure and leaning in as far as I could, pushed everything under the surface with the shovel. It would probably still rise to the surface, I thought, but it would be harder to see. I placed the covers back and wiped the shovel on a nearby thin blanket. It was then I heard it.

A scuffing sound and a slight movement, enough to catch my eye. I hadn't seen him before. With his emaciated face and drawn back eyes like most in Auschwitz, he must have seen everything from the shadows. He looked behind him, for an escape, but I was on him in panic.

He had no power in his body, he was just a boy. "I didn't see anything," he cried. I dragged him from his hiding place and saw the fear in his face. "Please, make it quick," he whimpered. He assumed I was going to kill him. It broke the moment. "Go! If you tell anyone, I will kill you!" I told him firmly.

I never saw him again. I don't know if the gas chambers later took him or if he succumbed to sickness but he was gone. I waited briefly, checking it was safe to leave, and rejoined my work detail. No one said anything.

I worried for a while about the consequences of them finding Pleva's body but I needn't have.

Within days, the occupants of the block had explored the latrine after someone stated there was a face staring out at them from the shit below. A block meeting was hurriedly and secretly called where it was decided they had to weight the body down until it was completely submerged; to declare its existence would be a certain death sentence for some if not all of them otherwise.

We discovered Pleva was not a popular figure with the guards either, they found his toadying attitude tiresome. No one it seemed was overly concerned as to his fate concluding he'd either been killed by a fellow prisoner or by one of the more 'pro-active' SS men when they were drunk.

Eventually, as the occupants of the quarantine block changed, the body resurfaced and an SS investigation concluded he'd fallen into the latrine whilst inspecting it and cracked his head open rendering himself unconscious thus drowning. The authorities weren't prepared to conduct a post mortem given the state of the body.

I'd killed a Kapo and my fear dissipated. When close to death you absorb part of it, I knew I could kill and that gave me a certain strength. I returned to Filip and told him, his face turned from misery to happiness but I could see the sickness was taking hold of him.

My brother made it through to March 1944, just two months after Papa died. After months at the camp, the cumulative effect of his sorrow, the realisation of our mother's and Anna's deaths, the brutality of Pleva singling him out for harsh mistreatment and the withholding of his meagre rations, combined with illness, proved too much for him and he passed away during the night.

Before he died, I held him for several nights not knowing if he'd make it through. I talked to him as he fell asleep, my fear was he'd not wake in the morning. But wake he did and, although weary, he made it through the next. He lasted just one more night after which the light went out in his eyes, a light that would never go out in my memory.

I recalled all the good times we'd spent together, a good child that grew into a fine man. I'd miss him so much.

I held his now lifeless body and I wondered how long it would be until I succumbed to the inevitable. I wished for a quick ending to take me out of my misery; an overpowering loss, my whole family taken from me. Why should I survive such a thing I asked myself but my father's words haunted me and forced me to resist and fight. I swore I'd never forget a thing that happened in Auschwitz. I would tell our story and bring to justice all the wrongdoers.

I recited a blessing. "Blessed are You, Lord our God, King of the Universe, the True Judge..." I began. An SS officer walked in. I stood up, removed my cap and bowed my head.

"Look at me," he said quietly. "It's alright. Look at me."

I raised my head and stared into a set of ice blue eyes. He leaned forward until his mouth was close to my ear. I felt the barrel of his Luger caress my cheek.

"I know what you did," he whispered. "I know." He stepped back and looked down at Filip. My head was bowed once more. "Carry on, Jew," he said and left.

Later that night, I dreamt of flight, my arms lifting me into the air as a bird. I spread my wings and soared into the sky. All about me were the souls who'd passed on within Auschwitz, they all had wings as if like Angels. Up and up, we lifted into the night sky, above the camp and on to freedom.

It was a dream I'd have on many occasions in Auschwitz, one I saw as freedom and breaking away; it gave me hope in a world where there was none.

The loss of Filip was hard. I missed his companionship, we'd become very close, clinging to each other's company in the chaos of our world. I found myself crying at night. After his body was taken away, I knew I'd never see him again and that to me was unthinkable. Since entering Auschwitz, I'd lost my mother, sister, father and now my brother and in the ghetto, my grandparents. My whole family had been taken from me by the Nazis and I hated them. How could anyone ever endure this?

Chapter 5
Janis Ozols

On my return from Munich, I was greeted by my son and daughter as well as my wife Luiza. Apparently, I had no choice in the matter. Daniel took my bag from my hand and said he was parked not too far away whilst Lena began her interrogation of me.

"What are you thinking? You don't need to do this. My mother needs you at home," she said.

Luiza interrupted, "Your father has his reasons, I may not like them but I respect them. Now, leave him alone he's tired, he's had a long flight."

Lena was just about to go on so I interrupted, "I *am* tired and I'll hear none of your telling me what to do. If you want to know what I'm doing, come round in the morning for breakfast and I'll tell you," I said.

She started to say, "But this is not ..." I stopped in my tracks and held her cheek. "I love you, Lena, but please shut up, you're trying to overwhelm me and I won't put up with it." She tried again and I told her firmly, "Shut up now!" She was clearly shocked, she wasn't used to me being that assertive; I'd never felt the need before. Their mother had dealt with the children when they were small, I'd been involved in my work and my dealings with them were really the 'nice' times.

Luiza had been both mother and father in the younger years but quite often she'd allowed Lena to control things. I accepted the trivial things but, just because it didn't fit in with her life, she would not dictate to me on this. She would learn to respect her elders, if Luiza could accept what I was doing, so could she.

Daniel, however, would just listen and gauge his opinion from taking in the facts, he'd have made a good policeman. He kept quiet, but I knew he was thinking through the situation in his own way. I preferred that manner of going about things; it was much less intrusive and more respectful.

The morning came too soon and Lena and Daniel both arrived in one car. They'd clearly spoken on the way. Luiza made breakfast: eggs, salmon and bagels. We sat down.

"Ok, I've a history to sort out with you two," I began. Lena went to interrupt but I cut her short. "Listen, if you're going to keep interrupting me I'll send you away and just tell Daniel. Now be quiet," I warned. I thought it best to cut to the chase because Lena would just keep going until I lost patience.

"I was a prisoner in Auschwitz camp, my mother, father, brother and sister all died there." A silence came across the room. "I was tortured, beaten and my life was taken from me and I only got it back when I met your mother in 1955." I saw her movement. "I've not finished, Lena, so please keep your mouth closed whilst I explain everything." I paused. She was still and silent.

"I held my brother, Filip, in my arms as he died. He was just twenty years of age and my best friend. My mother and little sister, Anna, went to the gas chambers upon arrival at Auschwitz and my grandparents died of starvation in the Warsaw ghetto.

"These are all people you know nothing of but they are all people I loved as much as I love you," I told them. "Finally, I'm doing this because I owe it to my family, I owe it to my brother and I made a promise to my father."

I began to lose my composure but Luiza jumped up and held me, it was enough. "My brother was growing into a fine young man and beautiful little Anna was only seven years of age when they gassed her." I held my hands across my eyes. "My parents, Antoni and Zofia were such fantastic parents, they loved us with all of their hearts and my grandparents Kacper and Alicja, well, they were the funniest people to us as children and they loved us also." I wiped my eyes with my handkerchief.

"In the camp, there were people called Kapos, overseers, they were prisoners receiving better treatment and food as an incentive to keep the rest of us in our place. Most of these people did terrible things to us, most of them were war criminals.

"A while ago, I was given a file by a man I'd never met before, and I'll be given five more. Each one identifying a Kapo that I knew because I was there. All I have to do is meet each one then confirm they are the people on file. I owe my family what I'm doing. This is not a negotiation with you. I'm explaining to you something I had to hide from myself to be able to be the man I am today. If I'd have let this continue in my life back then it may have consumed me *and* your mother and we may not have made it."

"Oh my God, you went through all of that and kept it a secret for all those years, for us?" Daniel said.

"I had no choice. If I wanted a normal life, I had to put what was in my past behind me," I told him.

Lena just looked at me, then she stood up, came over and hugged me. "I'm sorry. I'm so sorry the way I reacted," is all she said. I'd done what I needed to do so the children were off my back, now they would only assist me.

I phoned Markowski the following morning. I wanted to know what was next. He told me, "I've posted out the next file, it is being sent by FedEx, your expenses for Munich should be in your bank today," he said.

"But I've not told you my expenses," I replied.

"Then tell me now, I've put $2500 dollars into your bank account, if you need more I'll do it tomorrow."

"How do you know my bank account details," I enquired but he ignored the question.

"Janis Ozols, is your next target. You'll remember him, he was the Latvian block leader. Within the file you'll find all the information. He was a criminal and a known collaborator and assisted in the killing of 151 Polish prisoners, Ozols ran them to be shot in the back of the head by the SS. He was also known to have whipped frail inmates and kick them until life deserted them.

"He was a sadistic man, entrusted to brutally run the gangs that took the bodies from the gas chambers. Yet again, he was another that escaped just hours before the camp was liberated." The line went dead. He'd put the phone down on me. I wondered why he was so abrupt for a moment but having told me what he felt I had to know, I guessed he simply had no need of further conversation.

Janis Ozols was now my target. He would be living his life unaware of the near thirty years of work compiled against him.

The next day, the parcel arrived, Luiza took it and handed it to me. We both opened it and sat at the table. "Should I know what is in the file, Emil?" she asked.

"I think it best you don't," I smiled at her.

For some reason, I remembered being told all those years ago, "Trust nobody and keep your mouth shut." Although Luiza was my wife and would die for me, I knew opening her up to what was inside the file may make her vulnerable.

The idea was to do this on my own and drag nobody down with me if it went wrong. For the next few days, I'd read as I'd done before, taking in the whole file.

His new name was Matthias Wolf. He'd intended to return to Latvia but discovering it had been overrun by the Russians, he became a displaced person and headed for Austria, changing his name to something more Germanic along the way. He'd settled in Vienna and his survival instincts made him a natural for the black market. He'd done well and in 1948, he'd enough money to start dabbling in the newly re-opened Stockmarket.

By 1952, when the market had fully recovered, his investments had boomed and he formed his own company and lived a privileged life of luxury.

The file contained a photograph of Ozols in Kapo uniform, circa 1942, and next to it a modern Matthias Wolf. A public figure, his image was readily available. You could see he'd aged considerably but it was the same man.

The days passed quickly but I filled them researching and completing the gaps that Markowski hadn't worked out and I visited some old colleagues who were still pleased to see me.

"Are you still alive, Emil?" Rodrigo Almond, a detective of twenty plus years, joshed as I passed through the office. I'd come to see my old chief,

Cooper Collins. I'd worked with him for thirty years; he was old school and I was sure he'd help me.

I'd been through so much with Cooper. We knew each other well and had covered for the other's back on many occasions. "Hi, Coop, I need a favour," was my opening line.

He grinned. "You do know we retired you? What can you possibly want a favour off me for? Are you in trouble?" he enquired. I explained my situation; with him I could be honest and tell the truth, I could trust him.

I told him about Janis Ozols and the trade I believed he was involved in then asked if I could look at a cold case. Cooper gave me all he could and told me if I needed anything to just call. I still had my old police identity card, for some reason nobody had asked me for it on retirement and I'd thought my picture looked good so I'd stuck it in a souvenir box and forgot about it, until that is, I needed a plan for Vienna. I was going to use it to get me an interview with Matthias Wolf.

Aleksy Markowski had been researching into insider trading and hit a brick wall, but I'd found through some contacts that Matthias Wolf had used a trader to get information on a new company.

Founded in 1991, they'd started out in England and developed new technology for the mobile phone industry but needed investment. This is where Matthias Wolf had stepped in to invest a considerable amount in 'Seca'.

In September the same year, Seca Telecom split from parent company Seca Electronics and formed the Secaphone group of companies.

The trader who'd found out about the Seca deal, Brad Harrington, became of interest to the authorities. His actions were thought to have contravened the law and he was investigated for insider trading. Harrington died in mysterious circumstances and his case was put on record as unsolved.

Matthias Wolf remained a major shareholder in Secaphone. In the couple of years since they set up, they'd acquired several assets, spreading the network. Wolf had made millions off the deal and the investigation hadn't only stalled, it had virtually crashed and burned; their only witness no longer available to the prosecution.

I'd keep that information to myself, for use only if needed. It wasn't proven but I knew the nature of the man, he was a survivor and would do anything he could to get away with whatever he could.

On the way out, I slapped a few hands, promised I'd come for a beer with the boys and tentatively said I'd do lunch sometime. All round a successful visit. I'd got what I needed for my trip.

The flight out to Vienna left at 1910, an eight hour and fifteen minutes flight getting in at 0825 CET.

Luiza had dropped me off at the airport, kissing me as she left, her words humbling. "Go do what is needed, for your mother, father, brother and sister. I'm very proud of you, Emil, so very very proud." She touched my face in a loving way, turned and was gone. I knew she was hiding her tears and I felt bad.

I got to my hotel around 10am, the taxi driver saying the weather had improved. "You'll get 20°C this afternoon."

I decided to get some sleep and set my alarm. In my dreams I recalled life within Auschwitz and one, in particular, came to me out of the blue. I'd not heard or thought of it for fifty years but somehow it had always been there; words spoken by my father as we lay in our crowded bunk. "They cannot take away what's inside you, inside your head, they can steal possessions, property and all your belongings but they can't take away your education." I woke with tears on my cheeks.

I'd allocated a week in Vienna because I suspected Matthias Wolf would not be an easy man to nail down. The file gave me his home and business address but I was sure he'd be well protected by security. I had his office number so my first plan was simply to phone, announce my 'credentials' and request an appointment. If that failed, plan B was to hang around the cafes, restaurants and bars surrounding both locations in the hope he simply wandered in. I made the call. My German was sketchy so, after introducing myself, I established the receptionist spoke fluent English.

"I'm in Vienna on an enquiry Greenwich Police are making and my chief has now asked me, seeing as I'm already here, to speak to Herr Wolf about a simple matter that would help us close an old case and 'put it to bed' so to speak. I wonder if that would be possible? I'd appreciate it very much if it were. It'll take five minutes at the most," I enquired.

"Yes, I'll put you through," the receptionist replied.

"Hello, Matthias Wolf, how can I help you?" I repeated the information I'd given to the receptionist.

"I assume you need a personal appointment or else your chief would have called me himself?" He was very perceptive.

"That's right, sir. I appreciate you're a busy man but I need you to clarify something and, with respect, I could be talking to anyone, so it has to be one on one." I replied. To my surprise, he said, "10 am tomorrow is good for me. Have Kersti book it into my diary."

The phone clicked, the receptionist greeted me and I made the appointment. It had been easier than I thought it would be.

I knew there was always a possibility Wolf would have Greenwich PD called so I'd agreed with Coop that he'd personally handle any enquiries received and cover for me appropriately. If they asked after 'Detective Janowitz' he'd tell them I was. He didn't know I still had my ID.

It all seemed straight forward but I'd plan my interview, make sure I wore my glasses and make it a quick in and out so as not to raise suspicion.

Mid afternoon, I received a call from Zachary Perry, a solicitor working for Wolf. He was making enquiries about the reasoning for my visit. I wasn't expecting this at all, it was clear Wolf was now putting up a wall. I told him it was simply a case of putting things in order and closing the file.

"You've flown out from JFK to Vienna to close a file? I don't think so, Mr Janowitz." I improvised in respect of my non-existent 'main enquiry'. He came back with, "And what is the name of the local police officer with whom you are liaising regarding this matter?"

I hit him with, "There isn't one. It's unnecessary because I'm only here in respect of that case to research and reconnoitre. Look, I've just got a photograph I need your client to look at, that's all." More improvising.

"And my client would identify this person? I assume it's a person. In what context is he identifying it?" he continued.

"I'm working on a cold case that's been closed with hang ups which just need addressing and then we can put it to bed," I reiterated.

There was a pause. "With what you've informed me, my client is willing to be interviewed but it will be in the presence of myself," he stated.

"That's fine," I said, seizing the opportunity. "As I say, we just want this put to bed and there's no problem you being there, the whole thing will take no more than five minutes. I know your client is a busy man."

I put the phone down. "That was close," I thought. If there was doubt on his part it would have meant no interview which was all I was looking for.

I phoned Cooper from the hotel reception desk. "Hi Coop, I need a photograph sent through of a John Doe. I'm getting Wolf to identify it and it's the only way I can get a one on one, but I need it before tomorrow."

I gave him the fax number. "Leave it with me," he replied. "I owe you a beer," I offered up.

"You owe me a case full, buddy. I'll send it to this number within the hour. Take care, Emil, you crazy bastard," he remarked. The phone went dead.

I sat in the bar compiling my questions when the receptionist walked over and passed me the piece of paper. I checked the clock. Punctual as usual. Cooper had picked a good picture of a guy lying on the slab, eyes closed and hair neatly combed back looking like he was asleep.

I'd use this to suggest there may be a connection with Brad Harrington, a possibility of similar deaths – same date of death and same vicinity. I'd explain I was looking at whether we were dealing with a serial killer but if there was no connection between the two the case would have to be closed.

I finished my beer and walked into the town to visit the Museum Judenplatz, full of culture and contemporary exhibitions. I got a coffee and read a brochure, taking my mind off the next day's meeting.

I woke at 6.30 am and I went down for a breakfast of boiled eggs, cheese, ham and a croissant. I caught up with the news in English by picking up the 'Metropole' in reception. My preparation was done, I thought, no need to overthink it. I took a stroll into the city centre, a twenty minute walk that included the Danube but I'd still get there early. People were hurrying to work, busying themselves on mobile phones.

Vienna was a beautiful city. I made a mental note to tell Luiza that night about the wonderful buildings and architecture. It was a city I liked and was sure my wife would also but for now I was on a job, enjoyment wasn't what I was here for.

I walked into the office at Rotenturmstraße 14. Greeted by a receptionist, I gave my name and told them I had a meeting with Matthias Wolf at 10 am. I took a seat and waited.

"Hello, I'm Zachary Perry, I'll be taking notes for my client. May I see some identification?" He gave it a cursory glance and said, "Aren't you a bit old to be a policeman?"

I smiled and replied, "We're only a small department and homely with it. The chief employs some young people to do all the running." His hand came forward, we shook and he gestured me to follow him down a corridor, then up two flights of stairs and eventually into an office.

I noted how well it was decorated, the furniture immaculate, soft leather, clearly expensive. Perry offered me a seat and then disappeared into a door that blended into the wallpaper. Several minutes later, he reappeared beckoning me to follow him inside the hidden room.

It was deliberately dimmed and in a chair in front of the desk was a man who looked about fifty. My heart sank. He was nothing like the file photo. As I got closer, he looked like he'd had a face lift with plenty of work done.

I introduced myself and he returned with, "Matthias Wolf" then added, matter of factly, "Let's just get on with it, I'm a busy man."

Was this Janis Ozols? I needed a better view of him. "Ok, I'm going to need some light in here, I need you to identify a photograph but first can you tell me if you know a man called Brad Harrington, sir?" I enquired.

"Yes, I'm aware of Mr Harrington. He worked for me a few years ago. A nice man. He left my company on good terms and set up business on his own," he responded.

"Did you socialise with Mr Harrington at all and know of any of his friends or colleagues?" I queried.

"No, he was just a work colleague. I've no information to offer you with regard to his personal life," he stated.

"Can you identify this photograph?" I handed him the fax and asked again, "Can we have some light on here?" Perry put on the center light and as he did I focused on Wolf's face whilst he studied the picture, taking the opportunity to observe him closely.

The face had a leathery appearance and the brilliant white teeth were obviously false. His hair didn't look natural, his eyes tight as if pulled from behind and his nose was too perfect. I couldn't make him out.

"It's a man who passed away under similar circumstances as Brad Harrington," I informed him.

"No, I've never seen him before in my life," he said as I struggled to think of a way to delay.

Perry interrupted, "Well, that seems to have cleared the matter up. Is there anything else, Mr Janowitz?"

I looked at Wolf, I just couldn't make him out exactly, they'd done such a job on him and he could have been anyone. "Yes," I said suddenly. "I'm sorry to have to ask this but there is something in the main file concerning a man with a flower tattoo on his left arm. Unfortunately, I don't know what side of his forearm it was on, inside or outside, so I was just wondering if it would be possible for you to show me your arm, if you don't mind?" I was looking for the all telling Auschwitz number or a remnant of where it had been.

Perry was about to object but Wolf dismissed him impatiently. "I will show you my arm but then we are done." He rolled up his sleeve. There was nothing on the outside, no tattoo, no scar. The inside of his forearm was heavily scarred and it looked like a skin graft. Not the sort of thing you'd have done to remove a small tattoo. I had nothing.

I left the office escorted by Perry. "My client was involved in a car accident some years ago. It left him with serious burns. You didn't know?" I shook my head and he left me at the top of the stairs.

Desperately trying to think how I could identify a man I couldn't recognise I reached reception and suddenly realised I needed to pee.

There was a new receptionist and she directed me to a toilet nearby which I hadn't seen before because it was hidden behind what I took to be fake shrubbery. I went and peed then splashed my face with water, drying myself on the self dispensing blue paper towels. I needed to walk and think this one out.

Leaving the toilets, I stopped to check I'd zipped up, it was something I'd had to start doing having become distracted once or twice much to Luiza's embarrassment. It was then I saw him, striding down the stairs opposite, followed by an aide. I peered through the shrubbery, which was real but in need of a good watering. I heard him conversing with the receptionist then he left the building, his bagman scampering along after him.

It was him, the man in the file photo, the man in my memory, as clear as day. It was Janis Ozols. I'd started to shake with the shock. I hadn't been expecting it, somehow it made all the difference between composure and ... well, I was glad I'd already relieved myself. I took some deep breaths and, composed, casually approached the reception desk. She smiled up at me.

"I wonder if Mr Wolf is still here?"

"I'm sorry, but you've just missed him."

"Matthias Wolf?"

"Yes, he just left only a minute ago."

I thanked her and gave her my best smile. Whoever I'd interviewed, it wasn't Matthias Wolf.

Walking back past the Danube, I stopped at a bench and ate a sandwich I'd bought down the road. Looking over the water, I was pleased, it seemed to have gone wrong but my weak bladder had saved the day. There was no hiding it.

I rang Luiza and told her all I'd promised I would. I was on the phone for about fifteen minutes but I found it uncomfortable. I wasn't at my best and conversations on phones were something I'd never gotten used to; talking that long to someone that wasn't there felt wrong to me, I don't know why.

I spent the rest of the week going over my notes, spending time at several attractions and almost aimlessly wandering around the inner suburbs drinking coffee and eating the occasional meal.

I'd bought myself a pair of mini binoculars as an embellishment. I didn't know if I was being followed but, if I was, I wanted it to look like I really was a man on a reconnoitre and research mission.

My notes were quite extensive and I noted all I'd done and seen. If I say so myself, I was quite good at picking up the little things in life, like the fact the real Matthias Wolf had an accent. It differed to an Austrian one, it sounded like a mixture of Latvian and Nordic with Austrian added in – the exaggeration on the letter "S" was noticeable.

With Lukas Baur I'd noted his lack of respect for vowels, an Austrian trait. It would all go in the dossier. It was something I'd done in my work, the Greenwich police expected high standards and I gave them the highest.

I called Markowski and gave my information. It felt like I was reporting back to my chief but it was a brief conversation, he gave nothing away in his replies, I did most of the talking. He was happy with the identification and said he'd forward the next file immediately.

I managed to last the week and my return was greeted by Luiza. She'd convinced the children not to come, telling them I'd had a hard week, which wasn't true at all but the lie provided a welcome break from the constant questions from my daughter.

Luiza didn't ask me any questions, she just drove home from JFK and filled me in on a week's gossip – the dog had gotten into next door's garden on Wednesday, Daniel had an interview for a promotion and I'd have to call him when I got up tomorrow and Lena had a dental appointment on Thursday to which Luiza had to drive her.

I spent the journey quiet, in and out of Luiza talking at me. I nodded in all the right places, I think, but my mind was on what was to come, what the next file would hold and it was difficult to think of anything else.

I realised at that point, I really was doing the right thing. I'd had doubts, of course, I suppose anyone would, but in a short time I'd identified two Kapos. I know it was down to Aleksy Markowski's hard work over the years but I was now pleased he'd chosen me to complete his work.

I mused over how he knew me because I couldn't place him and I was good with faces. I decided to ask him next time I called.

That evening, my thoughts returned to Auschwitz, all the people who walked to their deaths or were beaten, the mass shootings, the forced labour and the starvation. I'd put all of it into the past and now it was back in my face. I was remembering everything, it was all coming back to me. Fifty years of covering up was slowly unravelling and becoming a part of me once again. What worried me most of all was when the job was complete – could I put it all away again?

That said, I slept well that night, no nightmares. Tiredness had overtaken me and a deep sleep came easily.

I woke late. Luiza had let me sleep in and then made me a special breakfast before the children came round when I let them know my updates. To my surprise, they sat listening with no interruptions. I knew then, at that moment, they were all on my side. I'd broken the back of fighting them to be able to do what I needed, my family were behind me now, I could rely on them.

I was a third of the way through the project and was determined I would find these remaining Nazi collaborators, determined they would know that Auschwitz had never gone away.

Chapter 6
Dante's Inferno

I struck him, he deserved it, stealing food was just not acceptable in Auschwitz. We were all suffering and you had to think of others, especially the weak and fragile like the elderly woman he'd stolen from. His name was Abner Lewandowski, he was in my block and he fell to the floor covering his head, anticipating a beating from me. It didn't come.

I just told him he should be ashamed of himself. The look on his face told me he felt guilty. He wasn't a bad man, it was the circumstances he found himself in. "I'm sorry. I'm so sorry, oh my god what have I done, what have I done?" he wailed. I knew his guilt would make him a better person; he wouldn't steal again, the shame too much to bear.

Since I'd killed Jarmil Pleva, we had nobody bullying us in the block and we ran it ourselves. We lived by rules, ones that were fair and we looked after the majority not the few. We had to have some normality – something to live by, not simply to survive under. We had meetings, food was rationed fairly, workloads also. I tried to instil a feeling of togetherness through which we could *all* aspire to get out of this if we worked together.

Although there were brick built blocks in the camp, ours was made of wood. Designed to stable 52 horses it now housed well over 400-600 people. The number changed as deaths and failed selections took its toll with new entrants frequently allocated.

It was hard after Filip died. I had to find a focus to keep myself alive. The workload we were given was detrimental to your health so you had to work as a team to be able to survive and I realised that straight away.

Controlling the block was difficult, theoretically there were just too many people but using the theory of tenths you could break down the numbers. If ten team leaders helped to let those below understand the rules we'd put in place, it was achievable. There would always be a bad egg in the bunch but we managed that in our own way, we weren't like the rest and we looked after the community, our community.

We didn't look outside our block. That was a rule we stood by, as cold and clinical as it seemed, it was the rule. The others could look after themselves, we couldn't accommodate any more. Each member of the block was spoken to at some stage by one of us. We were just normal prisoners but, at least for now, we were without a Kapo.

The rules were our reference point, they allowed us to have some control of our lives, each one of us knew them and the majority lived by them. And yes, there was a group of us, younger and marginally fitter than most and, reluctantly, we became the internal unofficial overseers. It had to be done.

A rumour had spread amongst some of the prisoners that I'd somehow killed Jarmil Pleva. I assumed it was the boy who'd witnessed it yet he was nowhere to be found. It was a dangerous time for me but, strangely, it somehow earned our barracks respect. There was less interference. Even some of the SS guards were curbing their whims in respect of our block.

Nevertheless, you couldn't take anything for granted. The SS didn't work together, they were random and sporadic and it seemed that's how they liked it – chaos a rule of law. One SS officer would shoot you, another would wave you by, that was the fear they instilled and you never knew which it would be.

Arvin Weisz was a tall man, his eyes were too close together, his chin was pointed, his forehead large, his head scarred and he'd broken our rules. He'd stolen two pieces of bread, a crime he'd pay for with his life. They didn't beat him or hit him, nothing so direct. They just sat on him until he could not breathe anymore. The system we put in place had broken down.

Suffocation is a dreadful way to die but better than torture. He died amongst his fellow prisoners, 'friends' he'd betrayed. I was made aware of his death shortly after. I went to the block and viewed his body, the perpetrators standing in line as if waiting to be shot. I shook my head. "There lies a body of a man killed for two slices of bread. Can we only deal with his crime this way?" I asked angrily. Nobody spoke, they all felt the shame but it was too late, he was dead.

His body was thrown on the pile, along with all the rest that had died in the night. I'd seen death in many forms but to be killed by your own people was a bad way to die.

By this time, it was difficult for me to ignore the gassing taking place and I understood my mother and little Anna had gone into those chambers. All I could do was think how scared my little sister must have been and pray my mother comforted her. The unthinkable had happened, I knew it now. I faced up to their deaths and got on with my life or what there was of it. I'd become hardened by it all, nothing hurt anymore.

The SS would visit us daily, inspecting our block, two maybe three of them. They'd ask questions and sometimes hand out a beating but mainly they'd just pass through because we 'overseers' did our job.

The hut caused them no trouble, so they generally left us alone, unlike other blocks.

Lice and rats were a big problem though and we would have to undress to be run to a distant bathhouse for occasional disinfection, no matter what the weather conditions. This often resulted in illness and subsequent death. Food consisted mainly of watery soup made of potatoes or turnip and a food extract I later discovered was made from weeds or fishmeal. Many times the vegetables they used were rotting. New arrivals often found it impossible to eat this muck but they'd learn; they had no choice.

Our working day would start at 0430, to the sound of a gong. We'd all rise and attempt to wash, defecate and drink ersatz black coffee or tea before the second gong sounded for roll call. This was when we'd make our way out, as quickly as we could. Every now and then it would turn into a 'selection' and for a short while there'd be more room on the bunks and less people waiting to use the open latrines.

You were just a number and a category to them: political prisoner, Jehovah's witness, Socialist, criminal, homosexual, gypsy and Jew. Everything was categorised, judged, scrutinised and abused. This was life in Auschwitz, an existence, no more than that.

One morning the SS were excessively aggravated, pushing people to the floor, kicking and beating them. Six of them, shouting and screaming, lined up twenty people and shot them in the head. We all kept quiet whilst they vented their anger and hatred, there was nothing that could be done. This was how it was, you kept your head down and prayed it wouldn't be you. From day to day, you just didn't know if you'd live or die. The SS would keep up their extra intimidation for a few weeks aided by the Kapos. Our block had to be extra vigilant, we had to make sure we didn't annoy them in any way; they were dangerous enough without us helping them.

Guilt was something I carried round with me daily, the guilt of having survived another day, the guilt of doing nothing. I knew I couldn't do anything but it still hung around my neck, a millstone that got heavier and heavier as time progressed. More than anything, it was my sister. I'd watched her walk off in her best shoes with her mother, her favourite doll in her hand. Tears came to my eyes whenever I thought of it. It wouldn't stop. I was strong for everyone bar her and she broke me every time, that little girl.

Twelve Latvian Jews were hung. Some unknown soul had done something to displease a senior SS man and a Kapo volunteered to choose victims. I'd never forget Lukas Baur. We all feared him because he had no principles, no morals and he didn't care how he survived. He and a female Kapo he was screwing picked three women and two children to be in the group to be hanged. Those two little boys were no bigger than my Anna and I would never forget their faces full of fear.

This atrocity was committed on the Hauptstrasse where the majority of us would be able to see them and they left them hanging for days, tongues swollen and protruding from their mouths, a deliberately macabre scene.

Life before seemed such a long time ago, so many dreadful things had happened since. We'd had a decent living, we were a good family and now all of that was gone and here I was watching men, women and children being hanged. What was a life if it was like this? Were the dead better off than the living?

Yet, there were flowers in the camp. Some of them flourished sporadically at the back of the blocks against the walls, little white snowdrops with their heads pointing downwards as if saddened and shamed by what went on around them. They were planted by an old man, under instruction of his SS guard, and though they were beautiful I thought they were out of place in such a world. Why would an SS man do such a thing? Was it done to torment or done in torment? It just seemed twisted to me yet, strangely, I still enjoyed seeing them. Analysing the Nazis was difficult.

Killing a man, as I had in Jarmil Pleva, came with consequences and, although he deserved what he got, I felt a deep shame for killing another. I'd taken a life, another human being. It wasn't easy to accept and I struggled with it from time to time but something was about to happen that thrust it from my mind for many years.

One morning, after a lengthy roll call, I was chosen with others to form a work detail whose job was to work the Judenrampe, the reception area for incoming transports. Our task was to recover luggage.

We formed up on the ramp. SS Officers and guards with dogs patrolled around us. We heard the train puffing slowly our way then, with a burst of smoke, it slithered through the camp arch and eventually came to a squealing, shuddering halt. A low moaning erupted from the cattle wagons behind the engine. The doors were dragged open and the SS began to shout, "Raus! Raus!" People tumbled out and were told to form up on the ramp.

Several SS men moved amongst them shouting in a language unknown to me. The man next to me commented, "They're Greeks." I asked him if he understood what was being said and he told me, "They're telling them their luggage is being taken for registration and they will get it back after they've showered." We went among them, taking their belongings, handing out little sticks of chalk to those who hadn't already written their names on them.

My co-worker helped me gather baggage which we threw onto a cart. I could see he was listening. "They're from Corfu. They're Jews from Corfu." I'd never heard of it. From the state of those on the ramp, gaunt faces full of desperation, fear and despair, it had been a long, long journey.

I glanced into one of the wagons as I returned for more suitcases. The floor of the carriage was layered in corpses: men, women and children. Those who'd survived had been standing on the dead. I stopped and stared.

Around me, dogs barked, constant guttural shouting and the sound of a whistle then in my head silence. Nothing. It was as if I'd gone stone deaf and, although I saw everything, I was physically uninvolved. I was there but I wasn't.

Abruptly, I was dragged back to the noise and the smell, the awful smell, as someone pulled me to a wagon and we began to pull bodies out and onto the earth around us.

Chapter 7
Miroslav Savic

We arrived in Lisbon at 0750. I'd decided to bring Luiza along as it was somewhere she'd always wanted to go and, after Vienna, I'd come to realise I'd have time on my hands. Anyhow, she was good company. Our stay would take up seven days.

The flight had taken longer than expected and it'd been difficult, my legs hurting after about four hours. Being confined in a small seating area was not good for me and the memory of a long forgotten train ride came back.

The file had arrived, as promised, and upon opening it, I thought to myself 'I'm not sure I know this man'. His name wasn't ringing any bells, initially. Miroslav Savic was described as a monster of a human being who used to enjoy the torture of his fellow prisoners.

He'd volunteer for punishment details and particularly enjoyed 'the Post' where he'd tie their arms behind their backs then hang them from a wooden post into which a hook had been placed at such a height that it was impossible for the victims to touch the ground. After he'd kicked away the support used to get them into position, they would dangle in agony, their only relief from the searing pain being if they could get traction with their feet against the rough hewn wood but this couldn't be done for long; the tearing of ligaments and rupturing of the tendons of the shoulder blades was always inevitable. He'd leave them hanging for hours. Unable to work anymore, their only future lay in the gas chambers. I couldn't begin to imagine the pain they endured.

He even took a pleasure in informing the SS of minor infractions of the camp rules, when many would have ignored them. Pointing them out, his finger became the ultimate betrayal of his own kind. I now recalled the man, his collaboration had no bounds. He considered himself above the other prisoners, almost as an SS colleague.

Luiza settled into the hotel and, unlike me, she didn't work out of a suitcase. Everything had to be unpacked and put in the right drawer or hung on the correct hanger. The hotel was nicer accommodation than my previous bookings because Luiza had chosen to not worry about the expense. After all, it was like a holiday to her.

After filling the tub with water and bubbles, she smiled and said, "I may be a while. Why don't you have a little nap?" I lay on the bed and closed my eyes.

A shape came towards me in the mist, fences surrounding us. My brother's eyes were deep in his head. He greeted me like he'd never been gone. We talked about our mother, how brave she'd been with little Anna and then I saw them, walking into the gas chamber, our sister looking up with fear in her eyes and Mother bending down saying, "It'll be alright, we'll just have a cuddle". She held on to Anna to the end, both of them clinging tightly to one another, past the last heartbeat.

Filip said to me "Here they are now, they've missed you so much," and out of the mist came Anna running towards me, smiling that beautiful smile. "Will it always be like this now," she said. My mother just looked at me with pride in her eyes, "You're such a good boy. I've missed you and your father's missed you." He suddenly appeared next to her. "I knew you'd be strong enough. I knew I could rely on you to tell our story."

In my dream, I began to cry. My eyes filled with salty water which trickled down my cheeks as we walked and spoke of the things families talk about. As I looked behind me, my grandfather was arguing with my grandmother but when they noticed me they smiled. "We are very proud of you, you are a good boy." It seemed as if I spent at least an hour talking to them when Father said, "We must go now." I said, "No, please don't go, please Papa. Don't leave me on my own." He tried to calm me. "You'll be fine. You don't know how strong you are, my fine baby boy." I pleaded, "I don't want you to go! Anna please stay! Filip no, no!"

The SS man came from nowhere. "Come," he said, quietly, and off into the mist they walked, slowly, waving. "We'll see you soon, don't be afraid," Papa called and then the SS man turned and looked directly at me. "Do you want to join them?" he said. I stopped and thought of Luiza and my children. "No," I said and he came towards me. "You're just another Jew, you won't be missed." There was no malice and he spoke matter of factly then drew his pistol, pointed it at my head and fired.

I sat bolt upright on the edge of the bed and tried to understand how the shutting of a bathroom door could possibly synchronise with my dream.

I told Luiza about it and she just said it was a weird coincidence but it'd happened twice now. Before, it was Baur and an early morning call. I wasn't a betting man so the odds may be somewhat skewed but it seemed like a billion to one chance to me.

My family were very much still with me after all these years, still helping and loving me. How intricate the brain is I thought, to be able to capture a whole family and store them for fifty years in every detail.

I'd read somewhere that plant life could communicate, apparently they mourned and felt loss. Communicating through their roots, they had an intricate system that we'd only begun to understand of late, or was it simply that time didn't exist in dreams which opened up more questions than answers for me. Shamans believed they could talk to the dead, communicate in some form or another. Is that what I was doing?

Luiza picked up a local tourist guide and sat in the room planning our week, whereas I had the file on Miroslav Savic. I'd studied it in depth whilst at home. What stood out was he had no family and seemed a bit of a loner. He worked from home it seemed. He'd been a salesman prior to this but it looked like working on the road hadn't suited him and, over a period of time, he'd isolated himself as much as he could from other humans.

I had his address and a bar he'd frequent when he crawled out from under his skin. Not a likeable type.

I clearly disliked him immensely. If it were not for Auschwitz, he would have found himself in prison for some depraved thing or another. I judged him as a deviant of some kind. His hatred of his fellow man was why he was a loner. He didn't like people's company, he seemed to hate it, and yet, he'd find the need to frequent the bar.

He'd been locked up in the '70s for a brutal attack on a woman who'd made the mistake of talking to him. He'd followed her, later that night, and attacked her, calling her a whore and prostitute. The hammer he used left her scarred for life and she'd been lucky to escape him. He was released from prison thirteen years later in 1986, returning to a sales job.

For a person whose people skills were questionable, to say the least, he was good as a salesman and appeared to have a knack for avoiding VAT without the consequences. It gave him a good life but he chose to live it alone, maybe the demons of his past were his company. I hoped they were.

I decided the bar he frequented in Lisbon was the best place to find him. A good decision it turned out because he was a man of routine and he'd go there at 5 pm every night, take a newspaper and read it on his own. If anyone attempted conversation with him, his cold response dissuaded further contact.

When this man died, I thought, nobody would miss him or attend his funeral. He was a horror of a man and the thought crossed my mind – why not kill him? I knew I could do it, I just didn't want the feeling of remorse, even for a piece of work like Savic. I'd feel regret, not for him but for myself. Though it would be hard to live with, Savic more than any of the others was someone I felt I could kill. The fact the others were killers and sadists like him was bad enough but he had something 'plus' about him, an oddball you could easily see as a serial killer.

I'd contact Aleksy Markowski with my updates but say nothing about my thoughts. I knew how to do it and, importantly, as an ex-policeman, I knew how to set it up and avoid the pitfalls. I had to admit it, I'd gotten myself personally involved in this case and if Luiza could read my mind she'd be in a frenzy but he'd gotten to me so much that it was now a serious consideration.

Luiza planned to visit the 'Time Out Market', a huge place that prided itself on street food in particular. As I'd planned to visit the bar Savic frequented in the evening, I could go with her during the day. She said she'd be fine in the evening, at the hotel, whilst I did what I had to do.

The market was stunning. Structured like a food court, offering different cuisines, the best chefs in Portugal ran small restaurants in the hall. Not too expensive, they had a fine selection of wines, beers and cocktails. Luiza enjoyed herself and tried some Lebanese food, observing that the lamb was cooked to perfection. I had to agree but my mind was thinking ahead to the evening and whether I'd get to see Savic.

Did I really want to risk everything I'd built up in my life for the likes of him? He just wasn't worth wasting my life on although I hated him enough to contemplate it. Who knows what he was like now; an old man with no friends and a dislike of humanity? His life must have been a miserable existence yet I couldn't feel sorry for him in any way. The man was beyond care. If they hadn't changed the law, he'd have deserved hanging with a short rope, one that would kill him slowly and painfully.

I walked Luiza back to the hotel. After three large glasses of red wine, she needed a siesta. I'd catch up with her later, it was time to walk down to the bar, Pensao Amor.

I sat drinking a beer taking in the décor of the former brothel which still had the imprint of its bordello roots. It was a surprisingly wonderful place with red wallpaper, leather chairs and curtains of a contrasting blue. The ceiling was a busy 'scrapbook' of classical nudes and on the stair was a painting of an old sailor smoking a pipe, the smoke whipped up into a cavorting scantily clad woman. There wasn't an inch of space untouched.

Two hours passed and nothing at all. I thought about Luiza back at the hotel on her own but she'd told me the night was mine, she'd be fine. The man who was regular as clockwork, according to the file, was not on time and it was looking more and more likely he wasn't turning up at all. The evening was a washout, a no-show.

I phoned Aleksy and told him so. He just said, "Stick with it, he's a stickler for his routine, there must have been a reason. He'll show." He put the phone down, abrupt as ever, but I was getting used to it. It was only the first night and we'd booked a week.

The following day, we took a tram to the Cais do Sodre rail station and then passed by the mouth of the Tagus river on the train to Cascais, a beautiful village, where the sun shone brightly on fishermen setting off for a day's work. Luiza loved it. "It's a bit different to our last holiday, Emil," she commented. I wasn't classing it as a holiday but I got her point.

In the evening, I again returned to the bar but, still, there was no Miroslav Savic. I had to curb my frustration. I'd been lucky before, I had a week and at some time he'd show. If I'm honest, I just wanted a visual to get the job done and then I could relax with my wife but I knew what was important, the enjoyment with Luiza could wait.

One beer turned to two and then more, before I knew it the towels were going on the taps and it was time to make my way back. I hadn't realised the effect four or five 6% beers could have but, even though I was a little drunk, the walk didn't take too long,

A warm night in Lisbon should have been enjoyable but I was frustrated. Where was Savic? Had something happened to him, I wondered? I thought about asking after him at the bar, gauging I'd get away with it because his personality was so putrid I doubted the staff would talk to him to let him know someone was asking after him. So, that's what I decided to do.

The following day, we visited the 'Praca do Comercio', an impressive plaza overlooking the water where we took some photographs just to show the children.

The history of the buildings fascinated Luiza, there'd been an earthquake in the mid-eighteenth century that had destroyed much of the place and what we saw was the rebuilt version. Lunch at the Café Central was a treat for both of us. The service was fantastic and we certainly made a memory there, one we'd remember for many a year. A walk back to the hotel at 4 pm along the river gave me what I'd missed the night before.

Time came around again and I sat at the bar half expecting a similar result. I got talking to the bar staff purposely, I had an agenda but, in fairness, they were good company. They were aware of the man I was looking for but didn't know his name; it had come as a surprise when I told them it was Miroslav Savic.

I thought, maybe he'd changed his name but it wasn't in my file. He'd be the first who didn't want to hide his past, such was his oddness.

Joseph and Amelia served me that night and they seemed to be interested in how my holiday was going. I'd give only what was needed but I saw no reason not to tell them of my day in Praca do

Comercio and Cascais, it deflected from my questioning about Savic's whereabouts.

They were unaware why he'd not come in. Maybe he was on holiday himself, they suggested. It was something I hadn't considered but he didn't come across as someone who took holidays. It wasn't his routine.

Around 9 pm, I was sitting at the bar talking to Joseph, about nothing in particular, when his eyes signalled I should look behind me. As I turned, a man was sitting down in a corner seat, glazed expression, nose badly bruised, mouth split, ears cut, left eye almost closed with swelling and the right clearly bloodshot. Someone had given him a beating or he'd fallen from a height into some sturdy bushes, either way, I had no doubts though, it was Savic.

I smiled at my find but most of all for the pain he'd been gifted. Joseph continued his conversation but I wasn't giving him my full attention. I was taking Savic in, enjoying the pain he was in. He must be nearing his 80s and to be beaten up at that age was a serious risk to your life, yet he'd survived and returned to his routine.

Noticeably, Joseph and Amelia didn't wait on him. They ignored him, such was their dislike of the man and, eventually, he came to the counter and ordered his drink. I noticed a limp and smiled at his discomfort. "Something makes you smile," he spat out as he stood next to me at the bar. I was taken aback but couldn't help returning, "Yes, but I'm not telling you." It didn't placate him. He continued, "Are you looking at me and smiling? Do you find me funny?"

I cold stared him back. "You really don't want to talk to me," I warned.

"Foda Se," (Fuck you) he replied.

"Likewise," I said, standing up and facing him. I was a lot taller than him and looked him straight in the eyes. If there'd been any doubt it was now gone. It was him. The adrenalin rushed through me.

I could kill him easily, I thought. I was still a reasonably healthy fit man and, looking at this specimen of a human being, he was nothing. I was confident. He stared at me but I never blinked. He faltered then broke eye contact.

Joseph realised the situation and broke the moment with, "Gentlemen, please, I don't want to call the police." Savic, under his breath, uttered "Foda Se", grabbed his beer and returned to his corner.

He left the bar after his drink, probably anticipating another beating he couldn't afford. I sat at the counter apologising to Joseph who, accepting my words, told me he wished I had thumped Savic.

I was pleased with the day's work, it had turned out well in the end. Two days of wondering and worry had been put to rest. I said my farewells and left but as soon as I got outside I knew he was there, I could 'feel' him somewhere.

On a spur-of-the-moment decision, I turned and walked off in the opposite direction. If he didn't take the bait, I could make it to a tram stop that would take me back to the hotel. After 100 metres, I knew he was still with me so I headed down to the waterside, just off the Avenue Ribeira das Naus.

Luiza and I had strolled along there earlier in the day and you could walk right down to the water's edge for a wide-open view of the bay.

As I hoped, at this time of night, it was virtually deserted. I ambled down to where the wet, paved gentle slope and the water met. I stood there, gazing out like a tethered goat, sure he wouldn't try anything whilst the occasional pedestrian and cyclist passed by.

I heard his approach, the scuffing of his foot on a raised edge and, from the shadows of the night, he came at me, wielding a baton as I turned to face him. I don't know what my plan had been. I wanted, at least, to confront him maybe even to beat him.

I avoided the first blow and he went tumbling past me into the shallow water. He splashed around as he got to his feet and came at me again. At that point, I called him by his name "Miroslav Savic!" I'd made my mind up, I was going to beat him.

He stood looking at me, "Who are you?" he growled. I replied, "The Ghost of Auschwitz, Kapo. Foda se!" He looked confused. I felt a strange calm come over me as I saw the fear momentarily flood over his face but then he suddenly charged at me, swinging the baton. I parried it with my left arm and hit him in the throat with all my strength, an open palm, fingers rigid and thumb splayed at ninety degrees. He recoiled, gagging, clutching his neck then staggered back into the water, turning as he stumbled against its resistance, falling forward into the gentle waves.

I stood and watched him, expecting him to get back up but he didn't, he just floundered there, face down spluttering until he lay still and quite lifeless. I could only assume the shore dipped away more steeply than I'd thought and he'd been unable to push himself up but, nevertheless, I could have saved him. Instead, I took a quick look around and decided, seeing as we were quite alone, to do nothing.

I realised what I'd done. Without really meaning to, I'd achieved what I'd originally contemplated. How long it would be before he was found I didn't know but it was apparent that the tide was now on the turn. If I was lucky, he'd be carried out into the bay and hopefully from there into the Atlantic. Maybe, he wouldn't be found for days and I'd be back with Luiza in Greenwich by then.

Being a loner, he'd have no family or friends to miss or identify him. It would be a simple open-and-shut case for the local police and his injuries, witnessed at the bar, would no doubt be connected and provide a useful distraction. I turned my back on him and rescanned the area. Nothing. Had there been an intervention of some sort, I could've rightly claimed self-defence. And, yes, I felt remorse, but I told myself he'd come at me which gave me the excuse to fulfil what I'd obviously wanted to do.

I brushed myself down making sure I looked normal for Luiza, she mustn't have any worries. Then, I calmly began my walk back to her, no public transport or taxis, just a simple walk avoiding interaction where possible. To say this had turned a little was an understatement but, as cold as it sounded, I thought at least I could spend the rest of the week with her, enjoying our stay in Lisbon.

I wasn't unpleased at the outcome. In fairness, they all deserved an ending like this but none more than Savic. To me, I'd served justice. I didn't consider what I'd done a crime although technically it was. I doubted he'd be missed by a single person.

I'd never return to the bar, the staff wouldn't miss Savic, life would go on without him, a better world I thought. If I was unlucky, he'd be found sooner rather than later and if the police made the bar connection I'd account for any of my DNA being found on him by inventing a mild altercation with him whilst I'd been walking back to the hotel. I'd check out a suitable route, one without prying cameras.

I returned to Luiza with an unexpected calmness about me but my night's sleep would be disturbed with images of Savic and all he had done in Auschwitz which, when awake, gave me a contentment that I'd ended his life.

I phoned Aleksy, telling him only that I'd information that Miroslav Savic was dead. "How do you know this, have you seen a certificate?" he asked. I responded by telling him his local bar had told me he'd passed away. I followed up by saying I'd been to his house, neighbours confirming the presence of an ambulance and that a subsequent check of local hospitals elicited that a patient of his name had been treated for a severe beating. Not convinced Aleksy pushed for more information, he wanted a death certificate.

I told him clearly I couldn't get that as they were only available to next of kin and I'd done all I could, the man was dead.

He reluctantly accepted my findings and we ended the conversation. I'd not let him know the truth, I didn't know the man and couldn't risk my future to him.

Luiza enjoyed the following day although she did say I was quiet. In fact, she informed me I was acting 'insular', which I didn't quite get but women say these things sometimes. I suppose I spent that day realising what I'd done but I filled it with a general walk through the neighbourhood, the purpose of which was, for me to find somewhere I could have interacted with him that was without obvious camera surveillance. Although she noticed I was conversationally distracted, Luiza appeared to suspect nothing.

The doubts remained but I'd killed before and knew it would pass. It wasn't like I was killing innocent people. Jarmil Pleva and Miroslav Savic had determined their future, two men who, upon death, would be visited in hell by the many ghosts of Auschwitz that they themselves had created. I hoped with all of my heart it was true.

But Luiza sensed something about me, she knew me inside out. "What is it Emil, something is troubling you?" she asked. I told her it was probably due to my search coming back as Savic being dead. I thought she half believed me but I knew she'd push the question until she got what she was looking for, in that respect she was very like our daughter.

On my return from Lisbon, Aleksy called me, he wanted a meeting. I agreed reluctantly, wondering what his reasoning would be. Had he doubts or had he somehow found out? Was the body found? Maybe it was just coincidence?

Then it really hit me. I knew nothing of Aleksy Markowski. I'd killed a man because of his file and his years of investigative work, yet I knew nothing of him other than he had an in-depth knowledge of Auschwitz and the people in it. I had no idea whether I could trust him or not.

The meeting occurred at the end of May and we met at the same location, the Bruce museum. Entering, he ordered the coffees and we sat and talked. His main reason for the meeting was clearly Miroslav Savic.

"What are you not telling me?" he demanded.

"Nothing at all," I answered to which he surprised me.

"We must have trust, if we do not have trust, we don't have anything," he stated.

"I don't know who you are Aleksy, you just turned up in my life with files and nothing else. You ask for trust when you offer me nothing," I said.

"You can trust me. Believe me, I have the same interests as you. I've checked on what you've told me and it seems Miroslav Savic is missing. Do you know anything about that?" he asked.

"I've told you all I know. The man was disliked by everyone, anything could have happened to him. He's dead, that's all I know so we move on to the next Kapo." I made the point, but I could tell Aleksy wasn't happy, there was something in his eyes that told me he didn't know if he could trust me. I wondered if he'd give me the next file and I was worried: this whole thing had absorbed me to the point of needing to complete the list, to fulfil the job.

He paused for a moment, weighing me up. It was something I didn't like. He pursed his lips and finally said, "He's missing, but all you know is he's dead?" He stared at me but I just stared back. Finally, with a sigh, he said, "OK, Emil. We'll move on but if you want to tell me anything at any point, you call me. You have a friend here. I may be an awkward man but I'm a trustworthy one."

He passed me a file, it was bigger than the rest, and told me to take a few weeks to read it over carefully. He suggested I'd need to take a break from this at some point and said now was as good a time as any. "Whether you feel it or not the psychological strain will be hitting you and you need to take some time to breathe."

I sensed he knew what I'd done and in his way he was posing the question *did I have what it takes to complete this without folding*? He'd spent over thirty years perfecting his files and gathering the information that was so critical to identifying the Kapos and I realised he was worried that I would buckle under the pressure.

This was now, to me, the most important piece of work I'd done in my lifetime. What I'd done with Miroslav Savic had been avoidable and had possibly put the whole project at risk so I decided to rein myself back in and do as Aleksy said.

I left him and walked home with the file under my arm, thoughts churning around in my head. How close had I come to being sacked from the job? I'd learnt the project was more important than any personal vendettas. Although I couldn't do much about it now, I did think I'd intimidated Miroslav Savic in the bar. Smiling at his pain, I had deliberately antagonised him and taken pleasure in it. I'd allowed myself to be personally involved but I wasn't too proud to realise my mistake. It was one I wouldn't make again.

Arriving home, I sat drinking a cup of ginger tea whilst I contemplated the next task. I'd be more professional this time. Luiza joined me in the conservatory, I'd forgotten her doubts and worries so I reassured her everything was alright. I'd had to learn to lie to my wife and do so convincingly. This was just something I couldn't tell her, it would destroy her if she knew she was married to a cold-hearted killer and, despite my attempts to convince myself otherwise, the essence of the thing was that the truth was the truth.

Killing wasn't easy. To live with it afterwards, you had to be able to square the circle and know that when you looked in the mirror a good man stared back at you. If you couldn't, you were in the wrong job or killing the wrong people and, at the end of the day, I could live with what I'd done, but that didn't mean Luiza had to. The best solution all round was to not tell her.

Chapter 8
Kanada

In the Warsaw ghetto, we felt oppressed and victimised but in Auschwitz it was different, it was survival when all about us was being destroyed. The change was massive and, although the ghetto was bad, Auschwitz was a living hell. Every waking moment was a form of torture, the slightest mistake meant death and you had to keep your wits about you, as I knew only too well. Luck played a major role in your life. Few could escape death here, not even the Kapos although they did their best.

When I killed Jarmil Pleva it was ignored, the SS didn't care – he was just another Jew to them. When Shyla Prosser attempted to kill the Kapo, Jacob Kreiser, his mistake was he didn't finish the job. He'd clubbed Kreiser without hitting his head, there were broken bones but nothing lethal, the failure to kill brought about his own downfall.

His murder was horrific and he endured the hanging torture for hours, after which he was taken to block 10 where they used him as an experimental subject; amputation with no anaesthetic. He suffered appalling agony and later gangrene took hold of him. Death was a blessing, really. His lesson was learnt by the inmates. Although people died on a regular basis, the fear of a death like Shyla Prosser's was enough to deter others. I kept a very low profile after his murder and, although I felt some kind of security, I took nothing for granted.

We learned how to survive in Auschwitz, little tricks that others wouldn't notice, like when getting your soup from the stockpot we'd always go to the bottom of the pan because all the root vegetables would fall there whilst others would hurriedly scoop away at the top because starvation had taken over. It was the difference between living and dying.

Dreams were filled with food, banquets, and feasts of plenty yet you'd wake up to the first gong with an excruciating pain but it wasn't your stomach hurting, it was your bowels. When your body breaks down, it starts eating itself and all you could do was get through until the next meal. By the second gong, if you had a drink inside you it dulled the pain.

Some wished for death, to end the misery. I had no time for such people. To me, they were cowards looking to be defeated and broken. I had a determination to survive for my father's sake. I'd made a promise I couldn't break and people who gave up, I thought, mustn't have had a father like mine.

The order of the day was different depending on what your role was. Working in the kitchens you'd be exempt from roll call along with the hospital workers. The working day was a minimum 11 hours but that was flexible and could be abused by the SS depending on what you were doing. Work details would often carry the corpses back of those who had died while labouring. It was a brutal life.

At 9 pm there was a gong and that meant night-time silence and it was adhered to, everyone by then needed sleep. The meals we were provided were of low nutritional value and bore witness to many deaths and crippling illnesses. Your store of fat used up, your body consumed your muscle mass and the tissues of your internal organs withered, followed by emaciation and starvation which led to a significant number of deaths in the camp.

If it didn't get you in the night, you could fall victim to a selection for the gas chambers. We *tried* to help one another but the stark reality was only the 'strong' would survive. As people in our block became too weak to eat, we re-distributed their rations to those who needed them most. It was a difficult decision but a necessary one.

When the little girl and her mother came into our camp, it was like the sun had turned to face me once again. As someone who felt so deeply about the loss of my little Anna, the small girl was a reminder of good times with a family but I hadn't initially realised they were together. On the ramp, the woman had wanted to know what was happening and I asked her if she'd had a job. She told me. One of the white-coated SS doctors gruffly demanded to know what we had been saying. I removed my hat and bowed my head, "Herr Doktor, this woman is a nurse." I was dismissed and the next time I saw her she was clinging to the child.

I took to them immediately; an innocent little girl, terrified out of her wits, being comforted by her frightened mother. Rohaan Emery had come to Auschwitz with her daughter, Meela, on the last train. They'd come in from the Lodz Ghetto and were more scared than anybody I'd ever seen in Auschwitz. I didn't know, at that point, that the father was disabled and had been sent for an early shower from which he'd never return. Hitler believed in the theory of natural selection and Toruń Emery found, to his dismay, that the only use he was to the Reich was to feed the crematorium. Such was our life, cold, clinical and efficiently utilised.

Rohaan had been chosen from the registration process because of her medical qualifications, she had skills that were needed. How the little girl survived I know not, possibly by chance they'd come across an SS man who found her too good or pretty for the gas chambers, so she remained with her mother. Many didn't. They gave Rohaan a post in the 'Schonungsblock' (the camp sick bay) and she'd later go on to be used in the camp hospital. In the meantime, I tried to help them as best I could and food was the obvious thing; the little girl needed it more than her mother.

Milos Pejic was a bully and a criminal. It wasn't known what he'd been convicted of but his tattoo told us he was a criminal.

Like me, often his work details provided him access to the camp sick bay. He took an unhealthy liking to Rohaan, following her and passing comments and she'd often be heard to say "leave me alone" or similar. I gave him a gentle warning.

"Why don't you do as she says? She's asked you nicely to leave her alone, so why don't you listen." I said to him.

His response was a chilling, "She's mine. I'll have her and there's nothing you can do."

Auschwitz created monsters like this and he was fixated on her. She was a pretty girl, even though the conditions of the ghettos and camp had taken their toll. It had with us all. The mess we were in made us all look the same and we'd been brought down to an equal level; gaunt with no hair. Sometimes, it was hard to decipher man from woman but I realised the danger she was in. I didn't know how bad a man Milos Pejic was but he looked an intimidating character. I might need help from the others.

On my own, I risked a conflict I may not win and I wanted to avoid that and all its consequences, especially after the attempt on Jacob Kreiser's life. Ironically, in Kreiser's case, the beating he took made him worthless to the SS and he was sent to the gas chambers, so Shyla Prosser had succeeded in his attempt but it had cost him an awful death.

In a low whisper, I voiced my thoughts that night and discovered the true situation. I'd been distracted and wasn't aware that Pejic was trying to ingratiate himself with the guards with a view to being appointed the next Kapo. A meeting of the team leaders had been called in my absence and the decision they made was he'd have to be silenced. No one was looking forward to him being the new block overseer.

I didn't feel it was something I should protest about. We had a block hierarchy with no discernible leader, a committee and yes, it was a committee of the strongest, those who had survived the longest, those who sometimes, of necessity, had to 'sign someone's death certificate' when it became obvious it was time to redistribute their rations. 'Benign' bullying kept the place in order.

I was there when it happened several nights later. After the final gong of the day, in the darkness, they hit him with a Kapo's baton, stuffed a filthy rag in his mouth and overwhelmed him. Then they sat on him until he breathed no more; tried and tested. His body was thrown on the pile of bodies the next morning, his face wrought in agony through the struggle he'd had, yet it still gave us a glimpse of a twisted grin, the face of a madman.

A possible danger had been extinguished, it was a sign of the times that normal human beings found it easy to kill another. When you're exposed to death on a regular basis and see it every day it becomes an almost natural progression.

Months later, one of the prisoners told me Pejic was convicted as a rapist and had beaten his victim, so what the others had done was doubly warranted. The perpetrators could feel appeased at the fact they had done the right thing, a life had been taken but they had saved us and Rohaan Emery from a fate unknown. Nobody mentioned his name again but Rohaan appreciated what had been done. She knew how perilous her situation was and that they'd saved her.

Within a short time, she became well thought of by the person running the 'Schonungsblock' and they allowed her to instigate early evening visits to administer to those not able, for one reason or another, to get treatment otherwise. Little Meela would accompany her and was a joy, especially to the older people in the block. In a place like Auschwitz, you took the joy gifted to you by the little things in life and to see Meela playing, as a child should do, lifted everyone.

After the light, came the dark and we were told by the SS to report to 'Kanada' – a thirty-block area used to sort the possessions brought into Auschwitz and, as funding for the Reich, never to be returned to the owners. Why Kanada? Because it was the 'land of plenty; if you were careful you could acquire things that might improve your chances of continued existence.

Our job was to sort the property left by the people from the trains. Left on the ramp, as instructed, it would all be taken by hand carts to a section where they would be sorted into numerous piles. Clothes, currency, gold, jewellery and all number of items were stolen from the people of Auschwitz, most of them already dead. We came to realise the scale of the operation the Nazis were working on and caught glimpses of the people being run into the gas chambers.

It was chilling to see, the disrespect for life, a disrespect we were now an active part of and, as I watched the souls run to their deaths, I thought of my sister and Mama. Kanada was a place where you saw the bigger picture. Fathers, mothers, brothers or sisters, lives that meant something to somebody, each and every one were now just part of a huge money-producing criminal scheme.

The grand scale of this was unbelievable; the annihilation of the 'enemies of the state', mainly Jews. Seeing it close up, as we could within Kanada, scared me. None of us would make it out of here. I knew then that they wanted us all dead.

We watched them, elderly men and women, mothers and children as they were herded down the ramp below the crematoria. No one ever came back out. We could, on many occasions, hear their screams and we breathed the air that stank of burning human flesh.

We were in a death camp; the culmination of the Third Reich's ambition to purge Jews and other 'undesirables' from the face of Europe. A biblical cleansing of my people was being undertaken. Returning to the block after those first days was hard – should I tell people how bad it was or not? It weighed heavy on me, would I just cause unnecessary distress and upset, what would I achieve? For the time being, we who knew said nothing.

Carrying large bags from the truck into the warehouse, we saw the little bird sitting on the perimeter fence chirping his little heart out, seemingly as pleased with himself as he could be. Observing from a respectable distance, he sat overseeing the horror before him. Although a twist of fate had swapped our positions, the bird free and man caged, we took pleasure in his visit. He was simply the loveliest thing we'd seen in the camp but, as quickly as he'd arrived, he flew off, back to his world. It was unusual, not just because of his beauty but because birdsong was normally absent from the camp, as were the birds themselves. It was as though they knew what was happening and feared the same outcome. Even the trees surrounding us seemed to whisper to each other, 'Shhhh'. You felt that at night, a strong feeling of nature turning its back on you.

We'd never see him again but we had his memory and, in the block at night, we would speak of him, the little bird that had given us so much hope.

Our barracks became a place of quietness to me *and* to the other members who worked at Kanada. I suppose shock had taken a hold of us all and we became inward-thinking. We didn't want to discuss it. For me at least, I couldn't get the image of people being run to their deaths out of my head, it was awful, something I thought I'd never be able to forget.

There were benefits from working in Kanada. Many of the new arrivals had food in their suitcases and bundles, expectant of a need for it, unaware of the awful truth; how could they be? We took advantage of their gifts, eating what we found in secret moments away from prying eyes. Some were able to smuggle small items out for use as barter, mainly with the Poles who were the only inmates with secret access to the outside world. The downside was the things we saw.

I was separating clothes: jackets, trousers and shirts, when someone mentioned, "Here's another!" We looked up and people were running towards the gas chambers. Another 'selection' had taken place. It would be the last time I'd look at the people entering the chambers. I couldn't believe what I saw, I felt as if my heart had been ripped from my chest. Rohaan and Meela were amongst the victims about to be murdered – the child and her mother, naked like the rest.

My legs gave way and I fell to my knees, gasping and sobbing at the same time, knowing the only outcome. Her mother comforting her, the life of the little girl who had given so much joy to our block was about to be extinguished. How could a child be a threat to the Nazis? I thought I would die myself then suddenly air rushed into my lungs and a wild howl came from nowhere. I covered my ears and wept, knowing by now how long it would take until their suffering was over. I said a prayer and stared at the earth, wishing for it to open up and swallow me.

Everyone else quietly turned and went back to work. Even the Kapo left me alone.

They murdered Rohaan and Meela Emery for no reason, no sane reason whatsoever. I'd thought Rohaan was a needed person. They were both needed, especially by me. But, the reality was nobody was *needed* in Auschwitz.

The barracks was an even sadder place to be that night. A little girl, loved by many people. She'd be missed by the lives she'd touched. I was hollow inside.

Chapter 9
Ludek Hulka

I took a break as advised by Aleksy. Anyhow, Luiza had planned a drive out to Sleepy Hollow in the Hudson Valley. The hilltop estate was famous for its beautiful gardens, sculptures, woodlands and streams: a relaxing break that I really didn't feel I needed, but I listened to advice and heeded the warning.

My mind was still on the job. Imagine reopening an actual wound. The cut being painful, you try to ignore it but the irritation's driving you crazy, well, that's how I felt with this situation.

My memories from fifty years ago were flooding back as I evolved into the task of identifying the six Kapos *and* all the awful things I'd attempted to forget, revisited me. Most mornings, I'd wake in a cold sweat. It was taking its toll but I thought I could handle it because I had to. I'd been through much worse and I just wanted to find an end to it.

They called it closure these days and it sounded good enough to me.

We returned from the break after three days, Luiza had enjoyed it. I'd deliberately not talked of the case so she could forget about it, at least for a short while.

Upon our return, I got a call from Aleksy. He informed me Miroslav Savic's body had been found. "Do you know anything about this, Emil? Is there anything you want to tell me?" he asked but I think he already knew the answer. I ignored him and replied, "I'm just going through the file. I remember Ludek Hulka."

Hulka was a Czech block leader, criminal and collaborator, like the others. As an overseer, he viciously beat his fellow Jews. Reports in the file accused him of being, 'the monster of block 7' and just like all their favourite Kapos, the SS had awarded him extra food and clothing plus visits to the camp brothel.

He supervised slave labour and sometimes, on work programmes, beat prisoners to death. In his file, the SS stated 'without Kapos like Hulka, the camp simply wouldn't function economically'. Yep, for the SS, he and his like were a great way of keeping the costs down.

This was how cynical the Nazis were, they'd use their victims to deliver the Final Solution, playing individual against individual, using people's fear and weaknesses against themselves.

Ludek Hulka was a retired head teacher. He'd spent thirty-five years working with eleven to sixteen-year-olds and my mind wandered, knowing what he was capable of. "Is there anything on file regarding him being a pedophile?"

Aleksy replied, "He took retirement whilst under investigation. They couldn't make it stick. The child in question, a boy of fourteen, withdrew his complaint." I knew it.

All the Kapos who came out of Auschwitz seemed to carry a disease: pedophiles, rapists and murderers, all deviants of one kind or another.

I'd been right to hunt them down. I thought of Luiza and what she had said about Simon

Wiesenthal and how, all of a sudden, I found myself on a mission to rid the world of them. No doubt, the two Kapos still to come would be a danger to society, in one way or another. Different characters in their working lives, but all similar as men.

Hulka lived now in Bucharest, Romania, and I'd begun to realise they'd all settled in cities and pondered why. Would it be to blend into the masses?

Maybe it was inherent in them, criminals historically flocking to cities because of the numbers. Rape and assault had lower arrest rates there and the lower probability of recognition was a feature of urban life. A report I'd read years ago pointed this out, explained by using victims' data.

It seemed these Kapos knew this and lived where they did for the camouflage – everyone could spot a weirdo in a small rural community but in a city, you'd be masked by hundreds if not thousands of strange characters. Around one per cent would be a danger to society, so by knowing these six men I was one step ahead of the game.

The job was talking to me, it had taken a while but I was thinking like a detective once again. I'd only done three years in uniform, made detective and never looked back. I managed to get promotion to Sergeant early in my career and I'd served as a field training officer, trained in all the investigative techniques including interrogation. It was a job I thoroughly enjoyed, even in the darkest hours I felt I was giving something back to society.

It seemed strange doing what I was doing now, re-utilising the skills I'd built up over the years and I wondered if that was part of the reason I'd been chosen.

I did my research, as usual. Ludek Hulka was a dangerous man who had, for many years, been in a trusted job, one which hadn't required a background check. The authorities didn't manage to think that logical step up until years later.

I flew out to Bucharest's Henri Coandă from JFK, arriving mid-afternoon, eleven and a half hours later. Situated in the south of the country, all I knew about the city was it had several large parks and a huge palace intended for the former dictator, Ceaușescu, but he never got to enjoy it because they decided to shoot him and his despised wife against a wall somewhere else instead.

It would certainly be on my list of things to do whilst here but first I had to identify Hulka. He was living in a place called 'Baronesse Center, camin batrani' and there wasn't much in the file about it which suggested he'd only moved in recently. I did a bit of follow-up work and found it was a retirement home and assisted living facility.

At just a fifteen-minute walk from the town center, it wouldn't be an issue getting there. I'd phone in advance, enquiring after him, telling them I was an old friend, I thought.

The phone rang, and after a few moments, the receiver was lifted. "Buna ziua, Baronesse Center, cum pot ajuta," came down the line.

"Hello, do you speak English? I countered.

"Din păcate, nu. O voi aduce pe Marie." The phone went quiet, several minutes passed and I thought I'd been cut off but then the line clicked and

I heard a muffled hand over the phone and a voice replied, "Hello, my name is Marie, how can I help you?"

I told her and added, "I'm an old friend but he may not remember me, it was a long, long time ago. My name is Emil."

"Mr Hulka is a resident yes, he has only recently moved in and he is a little under the weather at the moment. Did you say you are family?" she asked.

"Oh no, no. I'm just an old friend. How is he otherwise?" I inquired, with feigned sincerity.

"He is in general good health but his memory is not so good. He's an old man now, it is to be expected."

I wondered then if meeting him was a good idea, but why not I thought, so I asked. "May I visit him, I'm only in Bucharest for a week?" It wasn't a problem, she said and we sorted out the details before she continued. "Yes, I'm sure he would enjoy meeting an old friend, he doesn't get many visitors, just call beforehand. Why don't you come for dinner? We do nice food. Either way, I am sure he will enjoy the company."

I thanked her and asked, "Did you say your name was Marie?"

"Yes, just ask for me and thank you, Emil, we'll see you soon." She was gone before I could say my farewells.

Ludek Hulka couldn't have been that much older than me but he was already suffering memory loss; maybe dementia I thought. Age was catching us all up but, at least, I still had my wits about me. The file had been sketchy on his exact date of birth but he'd be maybe 80 now and I fleetingly wondered whether there was any point to denouncing him. However, to allow these people any thoughts of this kind was impossible. You had to remind yourself of the time when they'd been the men they'd been and I could do that. Finding them as OAPs didn't excuse what they'd done all those years ago and who knew what they'd done since? Anyhow, he'd had a decent life my family hadn't so it wasn't a consideration.

I called the home when I woke in the morning, letting them know I'd be there at 11.30 am. Marie said, "I'll get him ready for you," and put the phone down before I could ask how he was today; I wanted to appear friendly.

The walk from the hotel took in the Dâmbovița river then past the Tribunal Bucuresti court building which was impressive. Further on, down the avenue, a cut-through after a big roundabout took me through a housing estate and up towards the Virgin Mary Educational Center. Just a few yards further and I was on the Strada Eufrosina Popescu, the nursing home right in front of me, yet strangely invisible. I was turning around in circles searching for clues but not seeing it right under my nose. Down the road, I saw a local shop on the corner of a backstreet, high-rise blocks behind. I bought a bottle of water and a newspaper as props thinking they would assist me in being accepted by the carers and also Hulka; I wanted him to feel relaxed in my company. I showed the owner my piece of paper with the address on it and was taken back onto the pavement where they pointed to the spot I'd not long left. Only then did I see the building through the trees surrounding it.

Marie answered the door and welcomed me into the home, to the right there was an open door through which I could see several elderly folk sitting watching television. She explained they had individual flats in the home and took me up a set of stairs. Turning left along the corridor, she pressed a doorbell and I heard the sound of shuffling. The door opened and Ludek Hulka stood in a house coat beckoning us both to enter.

I greeted him with my hand. "How are you, Ludek?" I asked, touching base, testing the water. He responded, "I'm just fine, thank you for coming to see me. I don't get many visitors nowadays. Now you'll have to excuse me, I have what they say is memory loss. I feel fine but I just don't recall things, so they tell me." Convenient, I thought and wondered if somehow he knew why I was there.

Marie smiled that special smile carers have for old people and said to me, "I'll leave you together, maybe you'll take some lunch with us?"

"Yes. that would be lovely," I replied.

Hulka continued when Marie had left the room. "Now tell me, where is it I know your face from?" he enquired and I wondered if he actually did recall me or if it was just a polite response.

"I knew you from the old Bohemia days, way back," I told him. I was just about to say before the war then thought, no, I'll not give him a thing here, I couldn't risk him recognising me.

"Bohemia, I was born there," he announced. "I lived there."

As we spoke of things, he seemed to be struggling. The file Aleksy Markowski had on him had his life in much more detail than he could recall himself. Was I looking at a man who if I told him what he'd done he genuinely wouldn't remember? I thought I could ask him anything and it wouldn't matter if his memory was shot.

"What did you do after Bohemia, Ludek, where did you go? I've been in America," I tentatively asked.

"I lived in Bohemia," he said and I thought he was a lost cause but what followed took me by surprise.

"The family camp," he said under his breath.

"What's that Ludek?" I asked.

"After Bohemia, I.... I should have gone to the family camp," he said, trying to remember. I thought about what he was saying. Was he talking about the Theresienstadt family camp or another?

"Do you mean in Auschwitz?" I enquired, risking it a little.

"I was in Auschwitz, that's right," he recalled. "Awful, but I should have been in the family camp but the SS didn't allow me," he said. It didn't make much sense to me but I wasn't going to let that get in the way.

"I should have gone to the family camp," he said again.

I'd gotten something here, I thought. I didn't know what it was but if he wanted to talk about it I was happy to let him ramble.

"Did the SS stop you going then?" I asked.

"Yes. I had to go, had to leave Auschwitz. The Germans left and I had to go," he replied.

"Why did you leave, Ludek? Why did you leave before the liberation?" I asked.

"Who are you again? I'm sorry my memory is poor."

"I'm an old friend from Bohemia, the old days. We're both old men now." I tried to soothe him, not wanting to frighten him with his own memories.

"Yes, that's right you're from Bohemia. I've forgotten your name again, sorry."

"Emil," I said.

"That's right, Emil. I knew you in Bohemia didn't I?" he asked.

In a way, I did feel sorry for him, his brain was gone, you could tell him anything and he'd feel a part of it. I repeated, "So why did you have to leave when the SS left?"

"Oh, they didn't like me. They'd have killed me," he said with such innocence.

"Who, Ludek? The SS or the prisoners?" I asked.

"Yes, the prisoners. They didn't like me."

"Did you do something, Ludek, something wrong?" I gambled.

"Yes, I did. I did a lot of bad things." His look was sad and I thought I saw something I didn't think I'd ever see – a hint of remorse and guilt. I didn't push any further, I'd got what I needed; he was happy to talk to me.

"I did bad things. They told me to." He looked up at me with sad 'puppy' eyes.

I didn't want my head to go there so I said, "Ok, Ludek, that's enough for now. Shall we get some lunch downstairs? Come on let's take a walk." He instantly forgot our conversation, "So you're from Bohemia," he said.

"Yes, the old days. I live in America now," I said, soothing him.

We had lunch, chicken and veg I recall, and talked about meaningless things. His memories were there, they just needed the right person to bring them out. I thought of all those who had died because of him and I just couldn't connect the two people that were 'him' then and 'him' now.

I'd visit again and slowly gain his confidence. I wanted to know if he'd admit to the crimes I had in the file along with the witness statements Aleksy had gathered over thirty years. I thought it important to get him to accept his actions, even though it possibly wouldn't be admissible in court.

On the next visit, I took sandwiches I'd bought from the local shop. "Hello, Ludek, how are you today?"

" Hello, I know you, don't I? Did you come to see me this week?" he inquired.

"Yes, I did, I came yesterday. I'm your friend from Bohemia, Emil, remember?"

"Yes, Bohemia, yes," he said with a look of recognition on his face.

We sat and had a cup of English tea and ate the sandwiches. I tried to ease my way in on the questions, a cassette player in my top pocket on record.

"So, Ludek, when you left Bohemia, where did you go?" I slowly re-started the questioning from somewhere familiar, so as not to spook him too quickly.

"Yes, Bohemia, I lived there. I went to Poland." He was thinking. "Theresienstadt. I should have gone there, you know, but they wouldn't let me. I had a wife but they wouldn't let me go." he said. "The children died. All of them, all fifteen hundred of them."

It wasn't making that much sense and he seemed to be confusing one place with another but we'd get there, I was sure. I tested him, "Did you help?" I left the question deliberately open.

"Yes, I helped, but I did bad things," he looked towards the window as if looking for a way out.

I slowed it down. "OK, would you like another tea, Ludek?" He looked downhearted. "Tea, Ludek?" I asked again.

"Yes, yes please, that would be nice." I'd brought him back just in time. "And what did you do after you left Bohemia, did you have a job?" I asked.

"I taught children. I was a school teacher all my life. I miss the children, I remember them all," he said.

I felt his life was full of sadness brought on by his own acts yet at the same time, I realised this gentle, little old man was close to admitting some of his deeds. That first recording took a few hours and I changed the mini tape four times wanting to catch every moment but it looked like the week wasn't going to be long enough. I was worried I could interview this man for a month and not get all I needed.

I did the job as professionally as I could. Each day I visited, I'd bring a cake or a small something and we would spend lunchtime together; my plan being to go through the file, especially the ten crimes there were no witnesses for. Each day, I'd start over and each day he recalled a little more.

By Thursday, I'd surprised myself and covered the ten reports. I fed the information back to Aleksy, he was impressed. "Well done, we've got him on everything, with the evidence on file and your recordings they'll have to accept there's enough to prosecute."

I still felt a sort of odd pity for the man, even though I was listening to all of his crimes. He was making history. I realised that nobody could probably have been in this position before. It was unique, no Kapo had ever been recorded voluntarily admitting their crimes – there were Kapos taken and prosecuted for their crimes but that was different.

I listened, outwardly calm, as he admitted to personally hanging children, killing members of his block and assisting the SS in many of the executions. It was a long list and it was difficult to maintain a professional attitude at times but I found the subterfuge helped. Most difficult was sitting, looking at what seemed to be, for all intents and purposes, a nice little old man with memory issues calmly recounting such vile acts, occasionally with a small smile. He looked as if he was just another next-door neighbour, someone you'd never believe could do all of these terrible things.

I decided to probe over his alleged pedophilia, expecting it to be a question too far. "Your job, a school teacher, you loved it, didn't you? But you left it, why was that?" I asked.

Without a thought, just like he was throwing open the curtains on a sunny day, he said, "It was the boy's fault, he was far too beautiful. I couldn't contain myself any longer so I raped him. I couldn't go back. I resigned to keep my pension." It was as cold as could be, his main concern his pension. Then the curtains closed again.

Each time, I'd open up the box and get out what I needed then I'd close it with a cup of tea and a sandwich or a piece of cake and he'd return and forget all we'd talked of.

Often, he'd repeat himself again and again and a talk with staff at the home confirmed his dementia. It was difficult, much more difficult than the others. Killing Miroslav Savic was easy, so simple a thing to do compared with listening to a man admit all of this.

The staff loved him. He was new but to them, he was just a nice old man with a bad memory. How wrong they were, I thought.

Over the few days of visiting, Ludek got comfortable in my company, even recognising me and this was what I'd wanted. Getting into his comfort zone opened him up and made him feel at home talking freely. His reminiscences were important, proof of our life in Auschwitz.

Friday, I visited him one last time. I took two small cakes and the staff offered two cups of tea. We sat making conversation, him with a smart suit on and buffed shoes. Marie said he knew I was coming and had made a special effort so I mentioned to him how smart he looked.

"I always wore a suit for work, every day for forty years," he said.

"And how are you today, is your back any better?" I enquired, the day earlier, he'd complained of it.

"Yes, much better, they gave me a tablet."

I started on my slow build-up, "So what did you do after Bohemia?"

The morning went well. He acknowledged that, before the camp was liberated, a group of them had escaped. They hadn't a chance in the camp he said, they'd be strung up after the SS had left. I knew he was right. We had lunch again in the dining room and he said hello to some of the occupants of the home. It was a pretty well-run place, self-contained flats with a communal eating area and a living room where they could all meet, but in my head I thought, if Luiza ever puts me in a place like this I'll go crazy. As nice as it was it just seemed like you were trapped, an inmate. That was something I'd never be again and I wondered how Hulka felt about it or was the dementia hiding it from him. Being enclosed was something I couldn't bear. In the bathroom at home, I'd have to leave the door ajar. I didn't like closed doors, I suppose it was all a condition of my life.

"How is your holiday in Bucharest? You must spend more time with your wife," he offered, bringing me back.

"Oh, my wife is at home, she didn't come on this journey but she came to Lisbon with me a few weeks ago," I told him. Then he shocked me.

"Lisbon? I know someone in Lisbon," he said. He sat thinking about it for several minutes but couldn't quite remember so I put it to him. "Do you mean Miroslav?" His eyes lit up.

"That's it! Yes, Miro! He's a friend of mine."

I'd fallen upon something and I realised there was a possibility the Kapos had all kept in contact. I'd just assumed they'd all gone their separate ways. Had they always been friends after Auschwitz? I'd not thought to go down this route of questioning.

"He's a car dealer, he does very well. I'm all he has. He doesn't like people, they don't understand him, but I always have," he smiled at me. "I've not heard from him for about a year. He doesn't know I'm in here now. He'll come and see me though, he's my friend," he said, contentedly scooping up his vegetables with a spoon.

"Do you know anyone from Munich, Ludek?" I asked tentatively.

"Munich? Yes. Lukas. He lives in Munich somewhere. He was in Auschwitz with me." He fell silent then returned with, "We never went to the family camp, they didn't let us." The petals of the flower I'd opened in his brain were starting to wilt and fall so I decided to chance it.

"And Vienna? I went there a few weeks ago, do you recall anyone from Vienna?"

"Janis. I've not heard of him for a while." Momentarily, he looked at me suspiciously. "How do you know my friends?" he asked, quietly.

"I told you, I'm from the old days." I patted his shoulder in what I thought was an 'old comrade' manner.

"Oh, ok." He looked confused. "Ezra?" he suddenly said, as if he recognised me.

"No, I'm Emil, Ludek. I'm Emil."

"Oh, I'm sorry my memory is terrible today. I'm sorry."

I probed a bit more and he opened up about Janis Ozols. He knew all the Kapos I'd been sent to identify and they'd clearly all kept in touch over the years. I thought it strange, to do that. It was something I would have thought they would avoid and get on with the remainder of their lives, safety in isolation. But they'd all kept in contact, Ludek confirmed it.

It was my last visit and I left him saying I'd see him again, having more in mind a court date than a social event. As sorry as I was for his memory and the state he was in I just couldn't forgive him for the crimes he'd committed. The balance in his life could never be tipped.

I returned to my hotel room and sat for hours making my file notes. I'd done the same for the others. With Ludek, it took me almost four hours to collate all of what I'd learnt from my conversations with the Czech Kapo.

He'd offered up so much and I was able to take myself out of being personally involved with him, my Auschwitz was his. I'd found the ability to lift myself above the subject matter and be professional about the case. He had been different from the others. Where I wanted to kill Savic, I just wanted justice with Hulka. By no means did I excuse him. More than anything, I understood him and his ways because he'd told me why.

I realised he was a sociopath. If I told him to do something under threat he'd do it and have no conscience. When the SS had told him to do the awful things he did, he did them and had no guilt, because it wasn't in his nature. He would have felt abnormal to feel guilt. When asked why he did an act, he'd reply, "They told me," and then look at me like I had two heads, like "don't you understand." I always told him I did.

I wondered if they were all like him. I'd crossed this road before with Lukas Baur who'd shown signs of narcism. Did their 'conditions' make them do the things they did or was it what they'd been through that made them sociopaths and narcissists? What came first?

I thought about that all night. I'd been through much more than them and I hadn't turned – then again, I had killed Miroslav Savic and Jarmil Pleva which admittedly wasn't normal behaviour but I offset those actions with the fact I had guilt for both killings, not for the person but guilt for taking a life. I wondered where the line was drawn.

I'd considered myself a good man, I'd come from hell and survived it. I'd moved on with my life and made good, always believing in myself as a source for that, but talking to Hulka had confused me. As great as they were, the interviews did leave me a little uneasy. I thought of Aleksy's files and questioned myself. Should I be in there too? But then it occurred to me that, because I questioned myself, I wasn't a sociopath or narcissist and having the ability to question my actions gave me the freedom for the life I'd lived.

Hulka had taken me on a journey, not a pleasant one, but I'd learnt a lot from it. I'd suffered self-doubt and hoped I'd conquered it. I knew I was a good man, I had no doubts about that. But, after all I'd hidden, I had to wonder whether I was normal. I asked myself, why did I do that, hide from the truth? I'd always thought it was to forget my past and live normally but now the doubts were stalking me and I felt I was opening up like a badly sewn incision.

I'd lived a good life, I could say that now, genuinely, but clearly the balance was off and if I was asked fifty years ago I'd have said 'life had been good up until the Warsaw ghetto'. After that point, and before 1955, I would honestly say, my life had been awful. Millions had died but I'd been lucky, simply that, nothing more. Chance had given me Luiza and the ability to make my life better. It couldn't be anything else.

I asked myself a lot of questions because of Ludek Hulka but, eventually, I squared the circle. I won't say it was easy but self-analysis never is. I was a good man who came out of the wash, the Kapos were not and didn't.

Chapter 10
Winter

It became a living death around December 1944, people were dying where they stood. Muscle mass was none existent, bones were held together with parchment-like skin. Our barracks were almost empty, many had succumbed despite our efforts or had been forced to march to other camps. Only a small contingent of SS remained, intent on destroying the crematoria, the gas chambers and anything else they thought would incriminate them until, deserted by courage, they fled.

Roughly 7000 people were left to fend for themselves: the dying, the sick, the old and the overlooked, but we knew that at some point liberation would come and we'd be free; all most had to do was live long enough, not as easy as it sounds.

I was approached by a man from my block. "You should go, the rest will think you're a Kapo," he said.

" But I'm not a Kapo," I replied.

"We know that. We know what you've done in here, most of us are alive because of you. It's the other blocks, they've only seen you as the boss," he told me.

I was no Kapo, the insult upset me. I'd deliberately set out to help my barracks. I'd organised team leaders to help us survive and encouraged a sense of togetherness. How could they think that of me?

"You should go. You don't realise the hatred being dished out. Kapos are being murdered on the far side, retribution is being taken out on them. I'm telling you because I want you to survive. You're a good man, you've saved hundreds if not thousands of lives with what you've done. You should live," he said and I thought back to my father, 'Survive this and tell your story'.

I'd walked through the camp earlier, emaciated bodies and the dying all around, a human stain the Nazis had created, a vision from hell; even I was shocked at the piles of bodies stacked up. Before they left, they'd gassed hundreds, trying their best to disguise what they had done but the task and time had been against them as the Red Army closed in on Krakow. Distant explosions could be heard all around and the defence being fought lengthened our misery and pain.

My comrade and I were joined by two others. They had clothing in a bag. "Here, quick, put these on. We'll escort you to the gates."

"Come with me," I said, dragging the clothes on over my prisoner remnants.

"No. We stay. There are people who need us but you *must* go. You know why."

We bade farewell at the gates and I walked away from the camp, nobody was there to stop me. I couldn't believe it after all this time, I just walked out – it was that simple.

To survive, I initially headed away from the gunfire, it was the sensible thing to do, I thought. I walked towards Bochnia and came across no resistance. I kept going on the road to Rzeszow, sleeping where I could and foraging food whenever possible. Over the weeks ahead, I wandered almost aimlessly, finding solace in one place or another.

Months later, I found a newspaper and read how upon liberation many had continued to die because they were simply too malnourished. It saddened me, to be denied life after all they'd been through was just another cruel twist.

I had plenty of time on my hands to think about my life and it didn't take long for me to realise I had a chance, a chance to make a new start. I thought about all of the terrors that could destroy me and realised it would take time, I couldn't just shake the demons off.

Refugees were everywhere I went. In Przemyśl, I came across a group who had been liberated from Belzec extermination camp which had been built by the SS for the sole purpose of implementing the secretive Operation Reinhard, the plan to eradicate Polish Jewry – a key part of their 'Final Solution'. Like me, they were emotionally scarred people who'd seen more than life should ever allow.

I met a man called Lars Kowalski. He'd found work on a farm local to Przemyśl. He told me that the farmer and landowner, Pal Diller, was sympathetic, so I went with him and was received well and given a meal. Pal and Lars convinced me to stay and I settled in. At the time, I wondered how he could do it but Diller was a kind man and helped me; he could see what I'd been through from my eyes which were still set back making me look only a few steps away from death. "Stay, here. You won't get a foot in another door," he'd told me.

At the farm, I found out from Lars that Auschwitz had been liberated on the 27th of January, the newspapers suggesting over a million people had been exterminated and I couldn't take that number in. It was a number, up until that point, I'd not heard of.

The Red Army had lost hundreds of soldiers in the fighting around Auschwitz. Battle-hardened soldiers had been shocked at what they found within the camp and others. The hatred of the Nazis towards the Jews had them numb, according to their commander. I had known all of this because I had been part of it yet I found the reports distressing.

I'd started working on the farm thanks to Lars, his help was very much appreciated. My life had found its first safe port of call since I'd left Auschwitz and, for the rest of my life, that job on the farm would be remembered as the best job I'd ever had because it was day one of a new life.

It was a good living, the farm gave me a life I thought I'd never have again but I struggled with my memories. Leaving Auschwitz gained my freedom but opened up the mourning process. In the ghetto, you could grieve for your losses but within the camps, you simply mourned, there was a difference. Real grieving was a luxury you couldn't afford, the many horrors witnessed all went into a storage box in your head and you couldn't allow yourself more than a fleeting moment to think of anything other than self-survival.

Now out, it was an emotional journey. I'd seen so much hatred it had enveloped my life, pain and suffering had been a part of me and the blood that ran through my veins flowed with loathing for the Nazis. They'd killed all I loved and I was lost, inside, looking for opportunities for vengeance; it overwhelmed me.

It seemed the Nazis had camps all over Europe. Lars told me of the atrocities he'd witnessed in Belzec, how bodies had been exhumed and burnt on open grids. He spoke about the camp as I knew Auschwitz. They'd set about killing the remaining Jews in the camp and Lars only escaped by chance. The Germans, in a moment of sick humour, had called it Operation Harvest.

I was grateful for my new life and friend, never again would I take a thing for granted, each day was a blessing. I knew that, more than anyone, but I carried a weight, a burden, a pain that could not be exorcised.

Reports of the Final Solution kept coming. It had been a deliberate policy, the murder of all Jews within reach of the Nazis and they'd killed almost ninety per cent of Polish Jews and two-thirds of the

Jewish population of Europe. It was hard to take it in.

How could I understand what had happened? There wasn't any help other than talking with Lars so we exorcised our ghosts together. The only way of healing the scars was to talk it through. We both had experiences we couldn't cope with, our brains had shut down whilst imprisoned but now they began to let it all out.

Sometimes, the memories filled our eyes and rolled down our cheeks and sometimes they screamed from our mouths as we slept. The pain of the loss of so many loved ones was unbearable but we bore it, finding our own ways of dealing with a future without family. I became very quiet and inward thinking, Lars simply had anger and, over the years that we worked on the farm, it would manifest in his fighting with one person or another.

He was a good fighter too but seemed to enjoy taking the punches more so than giving them; I think he exorcised his demons amongst the blows. He became my best friend and we looked after each other's back – even after the war people had prejudices, spouting opinions that were just plain wrong, and we'd fight our corner defending the legacy we lived through.

Initially, many people flat denied the facts of what had happened, so much so that the liberating military authorities brought people from the local villages and made them witness the carnage, the bodies still piled up on carts. News reports showed pictures of villagers turning their backs on the sights they were being forced to see, shocked that this had happened on their doorsteps. They must have known, how could they possibly not have known what was occurring inside those camps? The burning pits and crematoria must have been noticeable from the stench of burning flesh. I read that one camp, Dachau, had villagers' houses virtually alongside its gates. You'd have to be blind not to know. They were collaborators, as far as I was concerned. Burying their heads in the sand didn't excuse them. They'd been aware of what was taking place and chose to ignore it. It disgusted and angered me, the hypocrisy of people.

I'd have had respect for them if they'd been honest, admitted knowing and said the Nazis were too powerful to challenge but there was no bravery to these people, they knew what they had done and now cowered in the shadows of their shame.

It didn't bring anyone back though. Slowly, I came to realise that carrying all that hatred would only bury you alive so I had to move on and find a way forward. Lars just kept fighting people.

I never returned to Warsaw or Luborzyca. I don't know why, it just didn't seem to be somewhere I could call home anymore and I turned my back on my career in the Policja. At the time, working on the farm, though hard, helped me in a way I couldn't explain but it *did* help. Maybe being outdoors was healing my soul.

Lars also came to understand working within nature and the outdoor life became like medication for us both – it had a calming effect on us. I think, at the time, we realised it was helping us recover and move on but years later I'd experience the same feelings on holidays, perhaps the countryside just has that about it.

They were good years, on the farm, ones I'd take comfort in for a long time. I stayed for four years and, in that time, I met many who had similar stories as Lars and I, people looking for answers and not getting them. The answer we were all looking for was unanswerable but it took many years to realise that. There was no answer, the Holocaust was a unique thing.

I left Przemyśl in 1949, wiser than I'd found it. Time to move on and find a life. The farm had been good to me, Pal Diller had treated me very well and he'd respected all of the Polish Jews and supported them in their time of need. He was a good man and I'd miss him. I asked Lars if he'd come with me, he'd been the friend I'd needed but his life was with his people and he'd a girlfriend, Panni. They'd decided to try to settle in Przemyśl. I wished them both well.

He'd been so important to me after Auschwitz, a colleague and brother, and I hoped I'd helped him as much as he had me. We had a farewell night, all the workers on the farm turned up, we drank vodka and sang songs, emotions were high and hangovers the next day plentiful.

On the road ahead of me was a world in recovery, newspapers filled their pages with Martin Bormann or Hermann Göring or any number of high ranking Nazis, endless tales, so many different stories.

The Nuremberg Trials had taken place and many of the senior leaders had been found guilty and some were shown the noose. Rudolf Höss, the commandant of Auschwitz, had been executed by the Poles in April, 1947, hung on a short rope outside the crematorium where he'd begun his killing spree of so many innocent people.

At the time of his hanging, I was unaware and still working on the farm, finding a way to deal with life and reading about his death, two years later, brought me some satisfaction.

My journey had just begun but I didn't know where I was going or how I was getting there. I just walked and lived from day to day, thinking the sunrise would show me the answer.

I went from village to village picking up work where I could but never settling. I passed through Kosice, Miskolc and then Budapest, where I worked in a kitchen for a while. Every new town brought me closer to a decision to settle but, inside, I could feel the journey was a thing I'd have to do to reach peace in my life.

Shaving one day, I saw the reflection of my arm in the mirror. The tattoo, 104627, stood out as if naming me and I hated it. They'd taken my name and thrown it away, replacing it with just six numbers, I wasn't even a human to them. I decided to get rid of it. I would not be reminded of this for the rest of my life, I thought. The Nazis had put their mark on me and I was free of them so the stain on my body was to be cleansed.

It was simple. I took a knife and cut deep into my arm, the pain tolerable, something I could withstand more so than the emotional torture of enduring those six numbers for the rest of my life.

The action of cutting my tattoo off my arm was a need, a purging of my past, done to free myself from what I was and what had happened to me. I'd never forget my family but I had to forget that, it was too much to carry. The wound scarred over but I was anxious the numbers didn't show through. I was prepared to re-cut it as many times as I had to but fortunately, when I eventually let it heal, they were gone. I'd done a good job. It was 1950, I'd spent four years of my life coming to terms with things and a year just wandering, looking for a revelation.

I now felt free, the world was open to me but I was still haunted by nightmares, yet inside I was healing. I left Budapest after I'd saved a little money, having decided to go to America. I knew if I stayed, I couldn't truly be rid of my past in Europe, everywhere I went there were reminders.

I'd arrange my crossing and attempt to make a new life, my decision was final. I didn't know exactly where in the USA I was going at that time but I knew it could only be better than where I was now. I had no doubts and threw myself into it one hundred per cent. If I could make it there and be happy, my past would be my past, to be forgotten. A new life beckoned.

Chapter 11
Anatoly Mikhailov

I'd learnt so much from my investigation of Ludek Hulka, Czech block leader and criminal, his apparent innocence just a mask hiding the true horror of his acts. It had been a successful session of interviews, the tape recordings invaluable. My report back to Aleksy Markowski was greeted kindly. The file was updated and, along with the other Kapos, it was becoming a substantial body of work, one I was proud of.

Anatoly Mikhailov was next on the list and I'd received his file in the post. I knew him, he was known as 'The Russian'. A big man and intimidating with it, feared by all, he was a political prisoner who wielded a baton like the brutal sadist he was.

Before his promotion to Auschwitz, on his own initiative, he'd locked seven partisans into a gassing van to impress his masters and earn 'points' towards his 're-education'. *They* died from carbon monoxide poisoning and *he* got a plum Kapo job at the Nazis' 'jewel in the crown of mass murder'. But that was just the start.

It was estimated he'd volunteered to work in the gassing of 89,000 able-bodied, disabled, aged and sick people.

His file was extensive, much more than I could believe and more than all the other Kapos put together. Like the others, there were lists of crimes and witnesses. Combined, the file I possessed had over two hundred written statements.

I was surprised someone I'd known could have done so much in his time in Auschwitz. I remembered him because he was the camp leader, the overseer of all the other Kapos, and he worked closely with the SS. The file told me the reason his body count was so large. It was simply that he'd been there the longest. Created by the SS, all who followed would be a mere shadow of him. He was the top man and had held his position right through the whole process of the Final Solution, from beginning to end.

It was around this time Luiza had a car accident. Entering a road, she'd been hit by an oncoming vehicle going the wrong way and she'd suffered a broken arm and bruising. She was lucky, it could have been so much worse. She spent a few days in hospital then returned home to recover, Lena took time off work to look after her and Daniel helped when he could but his new job was demanding. The Doctors said, for a woman of her age, she'd shown remarkable resilience, but then she'd never been a complainer.

Whilst she was in the hospital, I'd spent most of that period there with her and it almost took my mind off the file for a few days, but after she'd come home, it didn't take long before she eventually told me I was getting under her feet and ordered me back to work.

It was a relief if I'm being honest with myself, it had been difficult abandoning the investigation. Returning, I read something within the files which I couldn't stop re-reading.

Mikhailov had been in charge of the trains coming into the camp and led the separated groups to the gas chambers, lying to them to get them to enter the showers without panic. The rules said it was the duty of an SS man to administer the Zyklon B but Mikhailov was so trusted they allowed him to do it.

According to the file, he'd been in charge of this operation when I'd arrived at the camp, which meant he must have taken my mother and little sister, Anna, to the chambers and killed them.

Initially, I stood, staring at it, leaning over but not actually reading. I was oblivious to all that was around me and wasn't aware Luiza had come in. "Emil, what's wrong?" she asked.

"Sorry, I'm just....," The words failed to materialise. She came over and sat me down at the table, my legs were a little wobbly. "Luiza, I don't know if I can do this," I admitted.

"What is it, Emil? What have you discovered, is it something in the file?" she asked.

I took a deep breath and began to explain. "Luiza, this man probably killed my mother and sister." I held my forehead and tried to comprehend what I'd read. It had taken me by surprise, I'd never contemplated this sequence of events would turn up the killer of Mama and Anna.

"Oh Jesus, Emil. You need to tell Aleksy. You shouldn't do this, you've done enough. It's too personal."

I had to agree. I was lost within this now, my feelings all over the place and I was physically shaking. Running to the kitchen, I stood over the sink, waiting for the vomit to rise past my throat. It never came. I soaked my head with water and sat down.

I'd spend the next few nights trying not to think about Anatoly Mikhailov but inevitably he'd return haunting my thoughts, filling my dreams as well as my waking hours. I phoned Aleksy and told him what I'd found.

"At some stage, you were going to come across a ghost. It's how you deal with it now and how you move forward with this that matters. I can't ask you to do something you don't want to, but take your time over your next move, there's no rush. Don't make a decision you'll end up regretting," he said.

I think we both realised that the questions I'd ask myself over the following weeks would be crucial to the outcome of the whole case.

I spoke to Luiza in depth about the matter and she swayed on the side of not following it through. On the other hand, I was changing my opinion, I'd listened to what Markowski had said and not rushed my decision, it was too important and I knew I was the only one that could identify him. That single thing essentially made my decision for me.

I'd visit this Kapo for the sake of my mother and sister, that was my decision. I'd not kill him. He'd be charged with war crimes and have justice served on him because killing Miroslav Savic had taught me a valuable lesson. Although I'd effectively taken his life, his crimes were left unsolved and I was left with the feeling I'd let the victims down in some way. Justice had been served in a split second when it really should have been long and drawn out. I'd essentially given him the cyanide pill the Nazis had concocted for their easy getaway.

I couldn't possibly give up the chance to have Mikhailov brought to justice. He'd escaped from Auschwitz because he knew what the Red Army would do to him once they found out what he'd done – they'd have had no mercy. Luiza wasn't happy but again backed me, she knew it was something I had to do. Again, she'd help me book the journey.

Riga in Latvia, an uncomfortable trip for me, the seats just seemed too close together. I hated cramped conditions for obvious reasons; cattle were transported with more room. Another capital city, this time next to the river Daugava, whose old town had a reputation for being a beautiful, colourful center known for its art nouveau architecture and wooden buildings.

According to the file, I'd find Anatoly Mikhailov in St. Peter's Church which dated back to the early thirteenth century; renovation on the tower in the 1960s had added lifts to enable sightseers. A beautiful place, it towered over the city – who would believe within these walls of worship lived such a man. Ordained in 1959, he'd hidden himself as a priest, living a lie for over thirty years thinking his past was behind him but it was just about to catch him up.

I sat opposite, in a coffee shop – the square in front of me full of passers by and people eating lunch after a morning's work.

My plan was to talk to reception. First though, I wanted a recap on the file, I was sure I was missing something. Sipping my coffee, I was intrigued that he'd never felt the need to change his name. I rang Aleksy.

"No, I found nothing about a change of name," he informed me.

I let an exasperated sigh escape. "He must have, how would he have become a priest?" I enquired.

"Look, he may well have taken sanctuary. He's hidden his past well. He, more than any of our Kapos, had significant help. Let's put it this way, it wouldn't be the first time the church has given protection to a war criminal." He ended the phone call saying "Be vigilant."

It wasn't a Catholic Church anymore, poignantly it was Lutheran whose belief was that humans are saved from their sins by God's grace alone – "Sola Gratia", and their faith alone – "Sola Fide". If Anatoly Mikhailov had indeed been granted sanctuary within the walls then I'd probably have another barrier to break down.

He'd have studied scriptures for many years attempting to get God's forgiveness for his sins. I couldn't let it be given. He was a fake.

My initial thoughts were to present the evidence to the Police at the same time as all the others, the only thing with this case was the Church were involved so I'd need to present it at a higher level in the local justice system, the higher the better to avoid influences. I felt if I informed the Church it would only lead to Mikhailov being 'spirited' away.

I had a week to sort this problem out and didn't think it would be enough. It was complicated – to denounce him I'd be forced to do so to the

Archdiocese. In the Church, a priest may be dismissed from the clerical state as a penalty for grave offences but, to be honest, their track record in this respect was less than impressive. It was no use me denouncing him if the Church could cover it up. Nope, that wasn't going to happen, so now I had to be sure of what I was doing. The Church and its internal affairs could scupper the whole thing and Aleksy was aware of this – he'd mentioned whilst on the phone, "If he has the protection of the Church, we can't denounce him until the right procedures are followed."

I thought I might visit the local police station. I'd never come across a situation like this before, maybe someone could offer some advice. This case was different to all the rest, it had raised an issue that could potentially cause a huge problem in denouncing him, so I had to ensure I did the right things and made the right decisions. I didn't want Aleksy's work destroyed by a stupid mistake.

It was frustrating, to be so close and unable to do anything until you knew which way to turn. I knew

Aleksy just wanted me to identify and report back but I knew he'd gone inside the Church to protect himself from the outside world. It was a plan that could still work for him, if I messed up.

The chances of getting a case to court were low if you were protected by the Church, they'd not want the attention and would exert all the pressure they could. I needed to find somebody I could denounce him to who would be impervious to that kind of influence.

I went to the central library where an assistant escorted me to a computer. It was an IBM machine and he connected me to the net. Using a web page called Netscape, I spent over an hour researching my subject. I thought it was amazing how you could just pull up information like this. I found material on the Church and the Archdiocese and quickly wrote it all down on a scrap of paper. I'd let Aleksy know my findings later.

I told Luiza what I'd done. When I said we'd have to get one of these things she wasn't too excited.

"You'll be on it all day, Emil. Just stick to your books, at least they're real," she chided me.

Still, *I* was impressed, despite what she'd said. It was fast as well, not like the computers I was used to with the police – the pages loaded rapidly and I got used to using it quite quickly. Imagine being able to use one of these machines in the Police? Working on a job like the Ivo Fletcher case, it would have taken me a week instead of the many months of slog pulling all that information together.

I phoned a friend I knew at the Washington Post, a journalist named Dan Peachman, he'd worked with me on the Fletcher case. We'd formed a close bond and I had great confidence in his integrity *and* judgement. I asked if he had any contacts with reliable investigative reporters in Latvia and by chance he said he did, but he'd need to speak to them first to see if they wanted to get involved. When he came back with a name and contact number, he said he'd worked with them before and this was someone I could depend on. I called and explained Dan had put me in contact. Her name was Diana Russo.

I told her I had information on a person I'd located who was responsible for thousands of deaths in Auschwitz but didn't fill in the blanks. We arranged to meet up at the Vilhelms Kuze coffee shop.

Diana was a thirty something with long blonde hair and a great big smile. I immediately felt at ease and able to trust because she made a really good first impression and, anyway, Dan had told me he'd worked hard on a big exposé with her. I'd made copies of selected parts of my files, things that would help her but wouldn't give everything away – I was still a prisoner of myself, keeping things close and doing things alone.

However, I did let her know Anatoly Mikhailov, a priest of St. Peters, was actually a war criminal being actively shielded and that I couldn't rely on the church not to sweep it all under the carpet. *She* told me she knew a good, decent, honest man, Oleg

Valdemars, a first Lieutenant in the Latvian Police. She gave me assurances he was dependable.

"If this all goes to plan, Diana, you'll get a top story to tell your readers and Oleg will get a first class arrest, but I need you to both keep this on hold. It's important it all comes together at the same time. We can't risk the wrong people getting a heads up and doing a midnight flit," I firmly told her.

She agreed. I handed over the file for her to pass to Oleg and we parted ways. I felt confident I could have faith in her.

I decided I'd best identify Mikhailov. I'd gone to all this trouble and hadn't yet sealed the case and thought to myself, what if it's not him anyway, best make sure. I visited the Church again, this time I went in and made enquiries at the public reception. I asked about the priests, when would they be at prayer that sort of thing, just general information a tourist would ask. A lady told me they prayed at different times of the day, it was normal to see them at 0623 then 1213, afternoon 1356 and 1617 and finally night time at 1844. The timings were odd but then I wasn't a priest. I decided to come back at lunchtime, between 12 and 2pm.

In the morning, I sat in the coffee shop reading the file. He hadn't been forced to commit his crimes, he'd actually volunteered and, by doing so, endeared himself to the SS. At first, it was probably to save and improve his own life but later, as he became a part of the machine, he displayed all the signs of someone who believed what he was doing was right – he cleansed the camp of thousands of people and took pleasure in it.

The SS used domination and terror to rule the camps, they were able to run the camp with minimum staffing because of people like Mikhailov; they called it 'prisoner self government'.

As a prisoner, any contact with Mikhailov carried the threat of beatings and punishments of humiliation. He'd penalize whole groups for the actions of just one person. On top of the starvation and exhaustion, his psychological and physical torment caused many people to succumb to life threatening illnesses and, if you did, it *was* a death sentence.

His role in the camp was Lagerältester, camp leader. Directly linked to Obersturmbannführer Höss, implementing his orders, making sure the camp's routines ran smoothly, he'd recommend people to the SS for key roles as functionaries in the selection of prisoners. He had privileges: clothing, separate accommodation and visits to 'der Puff' (whorehouse). They were just some of his rewards.

He believed in the racial discrimination, bizarrely thinking he was superior and falsely thinking he was above the others in the camp yet, if he upset the wrong people, he could just so easily have gone to the gas chambers at any given point because he was a prisoner and nobody was safe in Auschwitz. But, he made sure he was an SS favourite and his knowledge of the German language had clearly helped his position. To him, being the Lagerältester was a career.

I'd seen him once, from Kanada, as he 'encouraged' people into the gas chambers, locking the door behind them then quickly running to pour the Zyklon B down into the rooms below. An ear against the door, he'd stood outside listening for the crying and screaming inside to become silence. After, he organised the work detail to empty the chambers of bodies and excrement. From where I watched, he was working for the Devil and enjoying it.

My memory was clear on Mikhailov. He was a vile human being who'd taken joy in murdering the innocent, his collaboration beyond belief. To volunteer to do jobs that would make normal people vomit showed how depraved he was – his hiding and 'seeking' forgiveness in the Church solely a hollow selfish thing.

Midday, just as the bells began clanging, I walked in. A deep heavy bell rang whilst birds that had fled the tower roof circled and called out in alarm. A notice board in the entrance advertised a concert to be held that night, 'Quiet Music Session' by Muza, a youth choir. It sounded good, I thought. It might be worth a visit.

I looked all round and could see several priests at the front of the altar kneeling down, giving prayer. It wasn't possible to get close to them but I got as near as I could, my Nokia phone had a camera, not brilliant but it took photographs. I took a number of snaps but doubted they would be of any use to me.

I stayed as long as they did, attempting several times to get closer to see their faces but it was no use, I was too far away.

I left a little frustrated but made my mind up to come and see the concert. Stopping in at the reception, I bought a ticket and asked for a seat near the front. Luckily, there was one left.

I'd spend the rest of the day seeing Riga's sights, taking the St. Peter's tower lift up to the viewing platform from where I could clearly see the 'Freedom Monument' and the red rooftops of the old town. Over to my right I could see the Daugava River. In the town, I visited a Latvian food tasting in the central market, it was relaxing but my mind was still occupied by Mikhailov's case. I couldn't allow him to be skirted off somewhere by the Church; he must pay the price.

I took a call from Dan Peachman asking how my meeting had gone with Diana and I let him know she'd offered up Oleg Valdemars as a policeman I could trust. He told me, "She may seem quiet but she's very good, you can depend on her totally."

Afterwards, I got a phone call from Oleg, a courtesy call. "Diana Russo has been in and seen me. I must say I'm intrigued, tell me a little of the case, so I don't have to go all the way through this file."

His curiosity already awakened, we talked for quite a while. He came across well and I felt comfortable with him, he seemed to me to be a man who believed in the law.

Later the same night, I went to the concert. I got there early to get my seat, settling in with a coffee. As people arrived, I watched carefully in case Anatoly Mikhailov showed his face. The concert was beautiful, the surroundings of the Church resonated with angelic voices and when I closed my eyes to listen carefully, I could feel the presence of Auschwitz around me, the voices echoing sorrow.

I'd listened to Henryk Górecki's Symphony No 3, early on its release around '77 and was blown away by its beauty, the three movements each had their own story. As a classical music fan, Luiza had introduced me to the work not knowing my past and it touched the part of me I was busy disguising. Tears would often fall and the music I was now listening to reminded me of his work.

I opened my eyes as the priests were walking past the stage. I eyed each one in turn and felt nothing until the last. I'm not sure whether the raising of the hairs on my arms surprised me the most or the sight of Anatoly Mikhailov. I'd convinced myself this was probably going nowhere and yet here he was, much older but it was him, I was fairly sure.

But that was the problem, I thought. The hairs on my arms were certain but suddenly the rest of me was in disagreement. I was only fairly sure and it wasn't good enough.

They sat down and listened to the concert. If he moved, I'd decided I'd move too but he seemed to be listening intently to the music. The distance between us now seemed huge and because they'd backfilled the empty chairs he was furthest away from me and not always visible. I'd bide my time, I thought, and wait for an opportunity to get closer.

Later, when the proceedings had finished, the priests and the audience stood up in appreciation then they slowly started to walk off and I had to make my decision. I pushed through the crowd to get closer and as he was just about to go out of sight, I called, "Father Anatoly! Can I have a word?" He stopped, which was all I needed, he'd recognised his name. His eyes found me and he said "What can I do for you, my son?"

I was now desperately improvising, pulling memory from the file; names and connections. "I wonder if you can help me? I need to find a priest from 1978. He was a friend of mine and I lost contact with him some time ago. The last time we spoke, he was here." Names were bouncing through my head. "Father Paulis," I offered up and smiled.

"I'm afraid Father Paulis passed away some years ago," he replied. "but may I ask how you know my name?"

I quickly explained, "Father Paulis spoke of you and to be honest I was just shouting in the hope one of you would acknowledge the name."

He seemed satisfied. "I'm sorry for your loss. I hope you haven't had a wasted journey," he replied.

I remained professional, but it didn't come easy. There were things I would have liked to have said but instead I simply told him I was in Riga on a short holiday and thought I'd drop in on an old friend I'd known many years ago, then thanked him as he said his farewell.

It was definitely him, the murderer Anatoly Mikhailov, I could see it. Now, I could say I'd not only identified him but that I had Oleg Valdemars on side to make sure, one hundred per cent, he didn't disappear within the system that is the Church. I walked back to my hotel, content I'd done a good job. I'd covered all corners and could relax. I phoned Aleksy and told him my news, he was more than happy.

"We've got the boss, the head man, it's all coming to fruition, all the hard work and stress. It will be huge news," he enthused.

"It's not over yet, we've still got one more to go," I said, quizzing.

"Yes, when you're back I'll arrange to meet you. The person involved in the next is important but I must see you personally so we can go through it together," he said and put down the receiver.

I read the file on Anatoly Mikhailov yet again, well into the night, reminding myself of all he'd done and completing my notes as was usual.

I fell asleep with the file on my chest, waking later to find its contents scattered over the floor.

Chapter 12
Luiza Simon

I met Luiza Simon in the February of 1955. I saw her in a bar called 'Frankie's' where they played great jazz of a night. I'd just finished a week's training with the Greenwich Police Department, a firearms course, learning the basics of handling a new pistol and, if I hadn't been on the 'end of course night out' with my colleagues, I may never have met her.

She was a nurse, studying for her exams at the time and a bit of a swot, I recall. I remember she helped a friend of mine that night. He'd taken a wrong turn into a fist, the owner of which got himself arrested having not realised his altercation was with an off duty policeman. To be fair, my friend was acting like a jerk and he'd deserved it.

He later let the guy go, admitting he'd been an asshole. It was the right thing to do, they shook hands and it was forgotten about. Troy Stephens could be a pain in the butt sometimes but he was a good cop, he just wasn't so good with a few beers down his neck.

Luiza had helped him with his bloody nose, cleaning up the mess and tending to his ego; she was a nice person. I thought at the time some guy's got a good girl there and didn't consider she was single. I'd find out she was too far into her studies to waste time on men.

She spoke to me when she was treating Troy, asking me to get some towels from the men's room. I duly went and she thanked me. That was my first meeting with Luiza Simon, a girl who would completely change my life.

Until then, I'd pretty much lived in a state of existence. I wasn't really connecting, I was turning up and making the effort but I didn't really know how to join in. After what I'd been through I was just ... there. Something had been taken out of me in Auschwitz but I didn't know that at the time, only hindsight made me realise my state of mind then.

I'd spent the remaining years of the 40's really re-finding myself and when I came to America in 1950,

I made the decision I was going to start a new life. At first I was totally lost, it wasn't what I thought it was going to be like, the streets were not paved with gold and it was just another place and a busy one at that. I soon realised that even though I'd moved to forget my problems, they'd come with me. I was trying to get rid of the issue the easy way, but it hadn't worked.

Greenwich had been somewhere I'd visited and I'd liked it that much I decided to stay a while. A free spirit in those days, it didn't phase me to jump from town to town finding employment here or there and, somehow, jobs always found me. I suppose the ghetto taught me to work hard and people always needed hard workers.

I joined the Police in 1953, needing steady income for my rent. I'd taken up an apartment near the center and the new job provided me with a colleague, Geoff Ryan, who took one of the rooms, helping pay the bills. We became good friends and would often frequent Frankie's bar on our days off. I guess after working a long week with all the cases we'd deal with a few beers really helped.

A regular haunt for me and Geoff, the night I met Luiza was the first time I'd been in Frankie's for a while. It was a good bar, laid out really well, a good old fashioned saloon you could say.

I noticed her sat in the corner, with a group of friends. I suppose girls do that protection in numbers thing.

She was what you'd call a 'Beatnik' kind of girl, that was the trend of the time, following the new music that was sweeping America. I didn't really understand much of that scene to be honest, I thought more about my past – my struggle with life didn't have time for things that were superficial. I probably came across as a bit of a bore but life wasn't easy for me. Outwardly, I looked perfectly normal *and* I was doing all I could to fit in, yet inside I was still in pieces. Geoff took a hold of me that day in Frankie's, as Troy and his new best buddy went to the bar.

"Ask her for Pete's sake!" I didn't know what he was talking about.

He shook his head in disbelief. "Just god damn ask her. She's single, you know. You keep looking, so ask her!" I looked doubtful. He laughed. "You don't have clue, do you?"

I remember giving some fool answer like, "She's with her friends."

Now, to be fair, I wasn't looking for a girlfriend at the time, at least not consciously, but I remember I was very taken by her. Geoff put his arm around my neck. "Listen, you idiot, she keeps looking back over here and I'm telling you it's not me she's interested in." He patted me on the back and told me to get two more beers and a shot of something to get my courage up. He then went to the john. I paid for the beers and a bourbon, turned around and there she was. "Hello, again," she said, with a smile that went straight to my heart. I found out later, Geoff had whispered in her ear as he passed her, "My friend at the bar really likes you but he's too shy to say anything."

We talked about nothing in particular and the more I looked at her the more I was smitten. We agreed to meet up another night and things developed.

Our first holiday together was in Sorrento, Italy, a beautiful place full of tranquility and sunshine. We'd visit Pompeii and Herculaneum, wonders of the world that took my mind off the job *and* everything else. The food was wonderful and it was there I found my love for seafood. The way they did that thing with pasta was just stunning. A whole new world opened up to me in the summer of '55. I'd experience things I never thought possible, a love of food and acceptance of emotions.

Considering I'd been starved almost to death some ten years earlier, I never believed I'd ever experience something like I had. It'd taken me a long time getting over the malnutrition, adding muscle to bone and I'd had a somewhat emaciated look for quite a while which gave me a hint of Sinatra when he was young and skinny.

At first, my body had rejected food but it eventually took it on, yet there were other complications with being malnourished and, for a while, illness seemed a long term consequence. Luiza wouldn't have looked at me twice if I'd shown up as I used to be. Somehow, good health sort of crept up on me, I just didn't feel ill anymore, the steaks and burgers had given me a strength I never thought I'd ever have again and it felt wonderful. That said, though, I'd never really lived as I did in Sorrento, being cared for by someone, enjoying her company, the food and wine.

Luiza told me, 'You earned it' but I didn't know what that meant at the time; I used to think it was just a saying in Auschwitz or the ghetto, one you'd hear before punishment was handed out. The Kapos used to tell us prisoners we'd earned what we got, that was my only recollection of that saying. Later, I took it the way Luiza had meant and never the wrong way again. It became something we'd never use in a negative sense.

Some years later, I saw a photo of myself and it shocked me. When you're wearing your body, and busy with trying to stay alive, you don't realise how bad you've become and I was no exception. Yes, I knew I was suffering but to see myself in such a bad way knowing I was one of the stronger ones made me understand how the people of Auschwitz really survived – pure luck.

It must have been 1958, the New York Times, it could have been anybody but I knew it was me. You know your own eyes. I was staring at my own photograph. I knew the others alongside me were ill, you could see it, but I hadn't realised I was as bad as them. When you look back on your life, most people have happy photographs and good memories but all I had was an accidentally seen picture, in a major newspaper, of myself in Auschwitz. It had been taken by someone who'd been an inmate, Wilhelm Brasse, and showed a group of men, all malnourished. My knee bones stuck out from my legs unnaturally, hands sticking out falsely attached to my arms, it was macabre. The man next to me looked no better or worse than me but he had his chest showing and his rib cage was just that, a cage of bones, mine was disguised by the smock I wore. I was looking at the camera as if transfixed by it. There were 23 people in that photograph, some showing anger, some fear, some defiance but most simply acceptance of what was to come, all so close to death they'd recognized the consequence, possibly even wished for it. I had no recollection of it being taken.

I remember looking at it just a few years later and thinking whatever happened to 'the 23'. Maybe I was the only survivor. These were my memories and I had to find a way of forgetting them.

Meeting Luiza in '55 was my epiphany, my moment of great revelation. I found someone who allowed me to put all of the bad things into the past. It wasn't her intention, she knew nothing of them but she gave me peace, something I never thought I'd ever find in my life. It was such a wonderful feeling. The love she gave wanted nothing back which gave me the excuse not to ever bring my past up. It was unconditional and I'd never had anything like it in my life. My parents and family gave me one form of love and I missed that so much...so very much my heart ached, but Luiza gave me another, a different kind of love, one where I was a student of myself. She broke my barriers down without knowing it.

I don't know if because of my circumstances I felt so much love from her or simply this was what everybody felt when they fell in love. I was like a young boy finding himself. Luiza was my Juliet and I loved the air she breathed. I watched every little move she made and it took me out of many a bad moment. She was someone who loved and trusted me. From where I'd once been I was high, as high as you could get. I recall the beatniks would dabble in certain drugs of that time but I never sought a false high, I had a real one and it was all I needed.

We'd spend time together, every moment we could. Life had opened up to me like I'd never known. Ten years earlier, I was nothing, The Nazis had wanted me that way and I obliged them, there could be no doubt of that, but I defied the odds, thanks to Luiza.

Over that summer we were inseparable, a deep friendship formed from initial physical attraction. I decided not to tell her about my past at that point, I didn't think it would help, things were going just fine the way they were, so I invented something acceptable. I hadn't been looking for a relationship but now I was having one and I wanted it so much. It had taken me by surprise and I'd have to say it was an amazing one.

Every now and again, in a moment of reflection, I'd feel a shame for enjoying my life when my family could no longer enjoy theirs. Yet, I knew if they were looking down on me they'd be enjoying watching me live my life, for them.

I *did* wonder how one day I'd tell Luiza, so much seemed unsayable, but I thought I'd scare her away with what was in my head.

On one occasion, I tried to tell her a small thought, a way into opening up but she'd closed me down not wanting to discuss the war. "It would ruin our holiday, talking of things like that," she'd said, not knowing.

I was still a brother and a son. I didn't stop being the person I was and I didn't stop loving them. As I grew older, *they* remained the same age, as if frozen in time. I never forgot them, I just forced myself not to remember. I chose to shut it out and eventually close it down – a slow process that coincided with getting to know Luiza, it had gone hand in hand as I changed my life. Luiza was none the wiser. I was good at disguising things. Our son being born was my first re-introduction to emotion at that level and it had shocked me how I'd felt. I'd hidden things away for 20 plus years, putting them in a box and closing the lid.

She accepted my invented past and never questioned me on it. Why should she? I'd convinced her I was the product of Polish immigrants, an only child, whose parents had died of influenza in 1946.

Now that I'd found a girl I loved, I feared losing her. I'd started a lie and I couldn't change it. I'd dealt with the unanswerable question of Auschwitz as best I could. What good could possibly come of digging it back up?

In my job, I dealt with death on a weekly basis, it was part and parcel of the work I was involved in. It was black and white to me, I was immune to the processes of murder or whatever way the body had gone from life to death. I had ways of dealing with situations that would shock other officers, but I could do what others couldn't because I had the experience they lacked. The only issue I had was with child killers like Ivo Fletcher, they made my skin crawl. It was just the fact the victims were children, like Anna, innocents that should have been enjoying life, not having it brutally ripped from them. Fletcher had done unspeakable things to Ruby-Leigh Cameron, just a little seven year old girl, and it sickened me that he had been trusted by Ruby's father. The poor man, blaming himself wholeheartedly for his daughter's death, later hung himself.

Fletcher gave evidence at his trial and specifically divulged things to upset the parents, manipulating the proceedings and blaming them both as he attempted to avoid culpability for his crime. Anthony Cameron had been a hard working father who, by poor luck, found someone he thought he could entrust with his daughter for the five minutes it would take for his wife to return whilst he took his tow truck to help a friend in need. The rest was a very sad, sorrowful story that ruined the family's lives.

Fletcher went to the electric chair and burnt. As the officer in the case, I attended and thought it would be a pleasure seeing him suffer, writhing in the chair. Usually, they put a brine water soaked natural sponge on the head, under the electrode cap, to assist the conductivity of the electric current – it aids a quicker death. Somehow, this time, they used a squeezed out synthetic sponge. Flames shot out from Fletcher's head and it took four attempts and nine minutes to kill him. I was reminded of the Nazi experiments the world was just becoming aware of and though I took no pleasure from it, he deserved what he got. The prison enquiry that followed exonerated the prison guards, blaming a problem with a supplier.

My sister was always on my shoulder in that case. She would talk to me in my sleep and tell me not to falter, so I fought long and hard to bring him to trial and see him executed. That night, I'd sleep comfortably knowing I'd caught and prosecuted a child's killer.

Even back then, Luiza knew nothing of my involvement in the case. Of course, she'd read about it in the papers but, seeing as the Chief had done all the talking, I was conveniently hidden behind the mantle of 'detectives investigating' and when she asked me directly I told her it was special squad and my office had no input. Early on, I realised I shouldn't bring things home with me because I'd open myself up to the big questions. I dealt with work in work time and my home life was just that. I didn't take the job home, I took my badge off at the door and became plain old Emil Janowitz.

All in all, at that time of my life, I'd found a home, one my mother and father would have been proud of. I prayed to them when I met Luiza, asking permission to see her, for them to give me a blessing. I knew they would have liked her. Often, my dreams would have Luiza playing with Anna and Filip, who'd always let them win. My sorrow was so huge that words cannot convey how I felt, but God had given me Luiza *and* a second chance to be happy. Although at times I struggled, I knew I had to concentrate on the present and not the past. To have those two things conflicting inside you is difficult to subdue but I wasn't like my brother, I wasn't hot headed, I was controlled and that helped.

For me to lose my control I thought was dangerous because I'd had a volcano of pain and anger inside. I was tested with Ivo Fletcher and I passed, though sometimes I wished I hadn't, but the end result was all that mattered and that's how I worked. If, for one minute, I thought he was going to get away with his crime I'd have snapped him like a twig but the law took its course.

It was March 1st, a day after the 28th when Luiza asked me to marry her. She said at the time she'd thought it was a leap year and we'd just have to get on with it because she wasn't waiting another three years. We were married in the July after a hectic period of saving money we couldn't afford. Having no parents to pay the bills, we both just made do. The ceremony was nice, the town hall at Greenwich was our setting, the ceilings were beautiful and, as we said our words, nurses, midwives and policemen sat filling the place but no family, like me she was an orphan. I remember feeling a regret, I wished they'd seen this, maybe they all still could.

Chapter 13
Ezra Farber

Back from Riga, I was met by my son – Luiza was in the car, her arm was aching so she'd stayed behind. A long tedious journey cramped up, the flight had taken its toll on me. I decided next time to go first class. I'd been buying tickets like it was my own money yet Aleksy was paying expenses and I'd done what he'd asked, so a first-class ticket was warranted, I thought.

I was an old man and I'd done more travelling in the last six months than I'd done in ten years. I was full of aches and pains after these long-haul flights. Things clicked where they shouldn't and I was aware I made a grunting noise when I stood up; being aware of your ailments doesn't stop them happening. Even when I got in Daniel's car I grunted a little as I sat down to greet Luiza. When we got home, I gave another groan getting out of the car and hobbled a little whilst I warmed my muscles up. I'd stiffened up during the journey and I was starting to feel my age.

I phoned Aleksy and let him know I'd got back alright, I'd already given him the news and was calling to find out when I was going to meet him again. He was a bit stand-offish and didn't tell me the name of the next Kapo when I asked, which was strange but from what I knew of him he was a bit of an odd guy anyway.

Going into a dizzy fit, Max greeted me like I'd been away for a month. His excitement was contagious. He brought me a T towel from the kitchen, pulling it from the drawer it was hung on. I often wondered what the hell he was thinking in his little dog brain. It seemed to be, "Here you go, a T towel, you'll love this! I've missed you." He was a great little fella and I'd missed him a lot too.

I took him for a walk to clear the cobwebs, it had been a long and tedious day, one I was glad was over. I knew I'd sleep that night for sure.

The next morning, I received a call from Aleksy. He wanted a meeting the following day but asked if he could come to the house. I saw no reason why not, Luiza wouldn't mind so there wasn't any issue with that. I asked if he'd like to come for lunch and we'd put a little spread on. He agreed and thanked me.

I spent the morning of his visit walking Max in the park and getting groceries for Luiza; some salmon and a few things she'd told me to replenish in the fridge.

It was midday as Aleksy manoeuvred himself around the coffee table. I could see the file, it was impressively thick. I thought to myself, *this guy must have committed some awful crimes.*

Having chosen a spot to his liking, he looked at me and nodded surreptitiously towards Luiza. I was going to say, 'It's alright, I've got no secrets from my wife anymore,' but the look on his face told me it was inappropriate. He wanted privacy. I asked her if she'd make a pot of coffee so we could talk alone. She smiled saying, "I'll be a while" and disappeared into the kitchen.

He started talking. "My name is Aleksy Markowski. I've never changed my name because I was proud of my family, they were taken away from me and I had to have some form of recognition of who I am. I spent time in Auschwitz Birkenau. I was just a boy of 14 years of age when I was taken from the Lodz ghetto and transported to Auschwitz on the trains. I survived the selection process, my parents went to the gas chambers and my brother died of malnutrition. My sister was used in the whorehouse. She died when she became of no use to the Kapos. The SS sent her to the gas chambers, then they burnt her body in the ovens.

"I went back to Auschwitz 1 from Birkenau and worked at the IG Farben plant in Auschwitz 3. I witnessed many executions and torture punishments within the camps. I was beaten on many occasions but I was lucky, I had youth on my side and an energy. Upon liberation from Auschwitz, the Red Army handed me over to the Red Cross who wanted me to resettle in Germany. I didn't want to live in a place where the population hated me, so I settled in Poland. There I became a student again and studied history. It was while I was studying that I read a book that mentioned a Kapo, in Auschwitz, presumed dead or so it said. That was the wording that set me off on a journey - 'presumed'. It was a hobby at first and then it became an obsession. I published a number of books, made some money and enjoyed a comfortable life but I'd spend every moment of my spare time researching the Kapos of Auschwitz. I found many had died but many were still alive. Over the years, I've compiled some seventy files on these people but some died whilst I was collating the information about them. Somewhere along the way, I realised that all I was doing with my work was taking all of the bad out of Auschwitz and I knew there was also good.

"You, Ezra Farber, taught people to survive. As a group, we listened and worked together and survived. Yes, I know you. I was in your block for a short period until I was moved back to the main camp. Many, many people survived that place because of you and the rules you taught us to live by. I call the files you have been working on 'The Auschwitz Protocol' because of the rules and codes of conduct you put in place to enable us to survive, not what the SS taught the Kapos to rule and kill by. It is *your* legacy. You helped so many endure at a time when we lost so many people. That's why I decided to make you the sixth file, to show the world that good prevails over evil.

"You are a good man, Ezra Farber, and yes, I know you. I was the boy who was hiding in barracks 10," he said quietly, looking over his shoulder in case Luiza was listening. "I was young but I knew what you'd done and the lives that one action saved. After Jarmil Pleva, I was moved to a work programme but I never forgot you. In your file, you will find hundreds of letters from survivors of your barracks. Not one of those letters calls you a Kapo, they call you Ezra and most of them told me about you in case I didn't know. You don't realise how much they appreciate what you did, they all thank you. The SS allowed you to take control because they believed in the survival of the fittest, and you were strong back then. I asked you to do this project because, like me, you lost your family and, like me, you had to find a way to survive. My way was to research the files and bury myself inside them, I guess yours was Luiza and your family.

"I know this is a shock to you, but you really were the only person that could do this. It's a unique situation but you knew all five Kapos, and being a detective also helped. You had the skills needed to do the job." He smiled. "I started reading about you a long time ago and have never found you to be a bad man. Our journey in life has been similar in some ways and in others not so, but I have always wanted the Kapos to face trial. When I got my diagnosis, I thought all my work was going to be wasted but the decision to add you into this as file number 6 was my best decision, and it was a way of balancing things up.

"At the worst time of your life, after losing your parents and brother and sister you didn't fold – you rose up and helped the block. You've probably forgotten how you rationed the food, the weak getting more and how you always told us to give a little now because when in need we'd get it in return. You managed the work details and protected us from other Kapos. You never took the official role of Kapo but in essence that is what you were and the other Kapos looked to you as an equal, but so did we. You helped the new entrants, as best you could, making it easier for them to adapt to the camp. After your brother died, instead of suffering, you took the role as the block leader and protector and we respected you for that and who you were."

He knew me. After all this time, he knew me more than my own wife. His file sat on the table, the name on its cover staring out at me. 'Ezra Farber', a name I knew as my own, a name I'd exchanged and forgotten so as to change my life. Inside my head, as Aleksy spoke, page after page had flipped over and over until the stark truth faced me again and I realised then that, on my return to Auschwitz, if I had seen the wall of prisoners, I'd have seen myself and possibly have not taken the job on. But chance had stopped that, Luiza had seen enough and my plan went unfulfilled.

It was all there, I'd witnessed the killing of the

prisoner by Lukas Baur when I was Ezra Farber. I recalled the file notes that showed, along with others, Ezra Farber often witnessing many other atrocities. The initial letter sent to me by Aleksy was addressed to Emil Janowitz but had EF scribed next to it. I thought at the time it was just a slip or perhaps something mailmen do, but he knew and was toying with me.

The other Kapos had escaped before liberation and I did the same because of a warning. I was told other blocks would see me as a Kapo and I wouldn't be safe, so I left the camp just hours before it was liberated. Because none of us had been accounted for explained why they thought we were dead, presumed gassed and why we were placed upon the wall of prisoners' life.

Aleksy had initially said to me that he'd found and personally identified one on his list and, with the onslaught of motor neurone disease, he wanted me to find the other five. His words had been specific, yet I'd overlooked them. It was me he'd found. Ludek Hulka had called me Ezra, which I'd ignored and said "No, it's Emil," but he'd recognised me, as poor as his memory was. I'd opened him up to his memories of Auschwitz and he saw Ezra Farber.

I should have put it all together before, but I was caught up in the moment, wanting to capture the monsters I'd known. I'd gone full circle on this, living the nightmare, getting through it somehow, making a wonderful life with Luiza and now the return of the truth.

She walked in with a pot of coffee. "I must admit I heard all of that," she announced.

"Luiza, have you been eavesdropping," I asked.

"I'm sorry, no, well, yes I did. At first, I was making the coffee and then I heard you were a 'good man' and I had to listen. I'm sorry but I couldn't help myself. I'm very proud of you Emil. I just couldn't stop listening," she replied.

"Have no worries about how good a man your husband is, Mrs Janowitz. He saved thousands of lives with his simple rules of survival without which they would have died. What he went through was awful but what he achieved was magnificent." He smiled. "He should be honoured righteous among the nations."

She sat down. "So you were a block leader in control of rations and work duties?"

"Yes, Luiza, but not a Kapo."

"You saved all those lives, Emil, and you didn't tell me. You should have told me," she said.

"I don't know what to say, Luiza. Memories fade but the scars still linger. I had so much happen to me in such a short space of time I just found a way that enabled my life with you. It happened and nothing I could have done would have stopped it but I had to change my life to be happy with you."

Aleksy interrupted. "The fact you survived Auschwitz and had the life you've lived is amazing on its own, but to be the only survivor who could possibly identify these five Kapos is nothing short of a miracle. I'm sorry I had to do this the way I have but I needed you. I couldn't risk scaring you off the job; my life's work relied on you completing it. But I want to ask you one more thing. I've given you five files I've spent years researching, extracting witness statements from hundreds of survivors but there are links I couldn't work out – the one between Anatoly Mikhailov and Lukas Baur especially, but they are all connected in some way or another. There was always a suspicion they'd escaped Auschwitz with the help of an SS man. Lukas Baur received money into a Swiss bank account, money that couldn't be explained. I've got details in another file, if you would investigate further?"

I looked at Luiza and she just nodded in agreement, knowing I'd want to do it.

"So do you believe this SS man is still alive?" I asked him.

He waved a finger at me. "Possibly. This is the connection I couldn't make; too many people were in the way, too many threats to my work. I accepted what I could and couldn't do. I had a moment, about the same time I thought of adding you to the files, where I realised I couldn't do everything, so I prioritised. I made notes if the information came about but I decided early on not to follow them up, I had to utilise my time efficiently. I can tell you that of all the suspects to assist Nazis to escape there could be no better suspect than Alois Hudal, a Vatican insider. He had connections with the Red Cross and, after the war, if he asked them to issue new papers, it would be done without question. However, I couldn't make a connection to Auschwitz. I do know that Lukas Baur had a contact when he escaped, someone who helped him with false documentation and I've always suspected Baur of providing the rest of them with financial assistance later on." He raised his finger again. "And, as you've educated me, that's probably why there is contact between them to this day."

"I'll be honest with you, Aleksy. I took this job on for the family I once had. I tried to escape my past and hide it but when your letter came, it intrigued me and, if I'm truthful, I was afraid of it. But being scared is not a reason not to do something," I told him.

There was an air of confidence about Aleksy, he'd known what he was doing all along by asking me specifically to research the Kapos. He knew I'd do it because of what I'd been through. He knew me, he'd researched my story, found who I'd become and trusted me.

The question now was when we'd bring the Police into this and open this up to the world – it all had to be timed correctly. Our Kapos knew each other and bad timing could send one or a number of them into hiding. We now also had the matter of an SS officer in the mix, but that was something I'd worry about later, right now I had my hands full.

"So should I call you Ezra or Emil?" Luiza asked, confusion in her eyes.

"Emil, the name we were married under," I told her. "My name is Emil Janowitz and it has been for fifty years. Anyway, it would cause chaos with our social life, we'd have a Mr Farber and a Mrs Janowitz, they'd all think we were having an affair." She laughed and poured the coffee.

So my name was Farber. I'd changed it for fear of reprisals. People were hunting Kapos down and killing them in the days after the war and I could easily have been taken for one. I wasn't ashamed of my name; I just had no choice, I had to change and survive.

How Aleksy Markowski found out I'll never know but he had and I couldn't deny it. I'd lived for nearly fifty years as Emil Janowitz and it seemed normal to me, my children bore that name along with my wife. I knew who I was and that was all that mattered to me. Events long forgotten had simply disappeared into the draw of history. The file I now kept hold of as a gift from Aleksy Markowski had witness statements all stating Ezra Farber did this or that, things I would remember upon reading but had forgotten over time.

As life moved on you forget many things but I'd always tried in my mind to act like my father was watching my every move. "Would you act that way if your father could see you?" I recalled asking Troy Stephens, my asshole work colleague. It was something I always did, act like I was being observed by my loved ones, never wanting to be a letdown in their eyes. My father's words echoed in my memory, "If it's the right thing to do, don't be afraid of what you are doing." Over fifty years had passed and I still recalled his words, funny what you never forget. As he'd told me, there are some things they can't take away from you.

For the next five days, I virtually lived at the Greenwich Library using their computers to research anything about Alois Hudal, including all the way back to his childhood. At the same time, I attacked it from the opposite direction checking every known SS man who'd been at Auschwitz. I checked Church records, birth, marriages and deaths and anything in between and beyond. The staff were great and one of them, Karin, being a German speaker even spoke to the occupants of dusty records offices when my German hadn't been enough. They were even making me coffee. By the end of the week, I was exhausted but I'd found myself a connection.

Chapter 14
Ernst Schaefer

The Church over the years had played a hand in the history of the Jews, this was the episode it played with the Nazis. They'd aided thousands of Jews within the sanctuary of the Church but also gave refuge to some prominent figures of the Third Reich.

I'd lay it all out on the big table in my study, planning it like a case file, photographs in front of me, place names, arrows linking who to who; there was a pattern to it all and I could smell it.

Although run for the Reich, Auschwitz was riddled with theft and pilfering by the Kapos and SS guards alike. With so much money, gold and silver passing through, it left opportunities to prosper.

There were several SS who oversaw us in Kanada but Hanning and Gröning were the two we saw the most. The two of them were not particularly diligent unless Oberscharführer Schaefer was present and they tended not to stick their noses in, preferring to look the other way, unlike the rest. We reciprocated.

Ernst Schaefer ran the Camp Admin and Accounting Office. A cunning, unscrupulous individual, he arranged raids on the lockers of those below him in order to catch them with contraband with which he could then blackmail them. He was detached enough from the others under his command to successfully claim ignorance of accounting staff pilfering and yet close enough to detect such, coercing those caught into turning a blind eye to his own illegal actions and generally getting them to do what he wanted. And if the SS sent an external auditing team in, which happened on occasion, he was in a prime position to deflect attention onto others.

Aleksy Markowski had found the connection to the priest. Alois Hudal was a supporter of National Socialism who'd written a book on it. He was the Nazis' link within the Church and he'd go on to aid many SS men to evade justice, amongst them some well-known individuals. Could he have done the same for the Kapos? It seemed unlikely but it was possible, especially once I'd found something which connected him to Auschwitz. Ernst Schaefer's parents were very religious people and well respected. They had known Alois Hudal well, so well in fact that they had asked him to be little Ernst's godfather.

It was all adding up; Schaefer, the camp, the Kapos and the Vatican. But why would Schaefer want to save the Kapos? Why wouldn't he just have them shot or gassed? It would have been so easy to do. I puzzled over this for days whilst Luiza supplied cups of tea and helped with the research; I gave her files to read, carefully removing anything that was disturbing to look at. She wanted to help.

"I need to do something, Emil. Use me to do the checking," she'd offered.

How could I refuse? I knew she was suffering just as I was. This nightmare life returning from the past tormented me and all I had let her do was watch her husband struggle. I realised she needed to be a part of this for my sake and it turned out to be a fantastic decision, possibly the best I'd made in a long while.

She'd been reading up on the five files and she ambled in with her head in one of them, glasses at the end of her nose, barefoot in her pyjamas.

"You do know three of these Kapos were in the French Foreign Legion together?" And just like that, it all came together in my mind. She didn't know it yet but she'd fallen upon the link that would tie them all together.

"Luiza, you're a genius to have found that. You've just come up with a crucial connection. How could I have missed it, let me have a look?"

"It was tucked away, beyond the main narrative, in amongst various papers detailing previous employments," she replied, smiling, obviously proud of herself.

I hugged her gently. "I think you may have established it's about comradeship. You little beauty!"

It made me wonder though, had Aleksy missed the connection or had he deliberately obscured it to test me? It didn't matter now due to Luiza's eye for detail.

Over the next few days, I concentrated my search on the Foreign Legion and discovered from a helpful person in their historical records section that all five *and* Ernst Schaefer himself had served together in the same small unit and, more importantly, they were all listed as having deserted on the same date in 1936.

They would have all known each other back then. I was certain of it; there was camaraderie between them! Records showed they all had criminal tendencies, possibly why they'd joined in the first place. When Schaefer had seen them come into the camp he realised the opportunity within his grasp and helped arrange their positions so that they could embark on a scheme to line their own pockets, the spoils to be divided after the war.

Schaefer, in overall charge of the currencies that were stolen from the prisoners at registration, was in an ideal position. The money and valuables the Jews had hidden about their bodies for future use to barter for their lives, hoping to escape the persecution of the Nazis, hoping to form another life in another world, all ended up at his 'feet'. He was a man who used his network of Kapos to further his desire for wealth after the war. At Auschwitz, his dreams came alive whilst for others, they died.

Everything was handled at Kanada and given to Schaefer by the sack load. I'd seen this happen with my own eyes. Every currency of the world went through his hands but only some of it was destined to reach the Reich. He ran a tight ship and controlled the entire accounting process whilst giving the impression of only a loose oversight.

My police training and nose for coincidence left me convinced. I'd found the link, I was sure. Ernst Schaefer was the connection to the process that allowed the Kapos to escape justice, an escape he could make use of himself; last known at Auschwitz, missing on its liberation, assumed dead in the defence of the West from the East, he'd walked through a cleansing fog of war and seemingly disappeared. I was learning things fast, beginning to connect the dots.

There was always someone who needed to ingratiate themselves with Kapos. The ones I'd known would point out to them people who had something hidden – money or jewels to trade or perhaps just a sentimental thing to be bartered as a very last resort and Schaefer's Kapos had cornered the market.

Things started to come back to me, like segments of a film played at fast speed. Images of the five Kapos; whispers in their ears, *their* whispers in Schaefer's. Beatings, seemingly gratuitously given, now making sense – a decent mouth full of gold teeth was always alluring. Beating someone until they were useless for work details might appear to be counter-productive to some but to Schaefer and his cronies it meant the gas chamber where precious items could be found and teeth pulled but not added to the thousands upon thousands extracted for the gold content; one for the puller the rest for the 'cartel'. I was pretty sure that's how it would have operated. There was everyday squalid opportunistic organised theft but this was more like hunting prey.

Schaefer was responsible for countless murders and I suspected now they were mostly for profit: gassings, shootings and hanging all took place under his orders and the Kapos were complicit.

My mind took me back to the day Rohaan and little Meela Emery were run into the chambers and had their lives taken. It was the same day we worked separating the items from the last train into Auschwitz. It was October 1944 and it arrived with 2038 Jews, of which 1589 were immediately gassed. The belongings were stolen and sorted in Kanada, the currencies looked after by Oberscharführer Schaefer with Anatoly Mikhailov, the head Kapo, and Lukas Baur alongside him. Between the three of them, they practically ran the camp.

Memories returned, I recalled things I'd seen but thought nothing of at the time but now there was significance to it all.

I was thinking out loud to Luiza: "Ernst Schaefer wasn't going to be caught stealing from the Reich, they'd have shot him and there was no coward like a Nazi coward. Why risk your own life when you had the Kapos to do it for you? If you could use your relationship with Alois Hudal in Rome to get them out of harm's way you'd have created an almost perfect crime, especially if you all knew who controlled the money." I wasn't sure if my wife followed what I was saying, but she knew not to interrupt my thought patterns.

Stealing from the thieving magpie of Nazism was a clever plan but had they pulled it off? It seemed to point that way. I had no proof but coincidence was a good friend of mine, he'd closed cases for me on many an occasion. If it looks like shit and smells like shit nine times out of ten, it's shit.

By now, I was totally immersed in this case; it had turned into something I wasn't expecting. My every waking moment was absorbed by research. I spent hours every day in Greenwich library, stopping only to buy a coffee on my way.

I kept Aleksy up to date. "Just give me a little more time, I'll get there. You've had thirty years to put this together but I've only had six months," I'd tell him. He wanted to go ahead with the arrests but, if we were going to get Schaefer as well, I knew I'd have to have all I needed before we took them in. I had to be sure and had to have my facts. There was no use arresting them without enough evidence to take down Schaefer along with them. I wasn't convinced he'd died in '45 and he was important to me personally. It was his regime that had killed my family not the Kapos; they were, for the most part, acting under the circumstances the Nazis had put them in. Real evil is the creation of a system of plunder and killing then allowing others to do your dirty work. No, I hated the Kapos with a passion but the real enemy was the creator. The final solution was created by the Nazis and Ernst Schaefer was one of them.

Whilst I wanted him, I wouldn't risk losing the others. They would be denounced in time. I just needed a bit of space to assimilate the puzzle that was unravelling before my eyes. For the first time in our life together, Luiza shared my work. She was obsessed, for my sake, and wanted an end to Auschwitz in my life, but I knew we had a chance here, a real chance of getting the thief of all thieves and taking down my five Kapos at the same time.

One thing I knew I was good at was putting together a puzzle; it was almost second nature to me. I'd done it a thousand times in my job. Aleksy had chosen well, I thought. "I bet he wasn't expecting this," Luiza would comment. I wasn't expecting it myself, up until now, but it was looking likely.

I was excited by what we were finding, for obvious reasons, but I was also sure of myself. I wouldn't mess this up, it would be my finest work. Cooper Collins would be proud of me, especially my newly found computer skills. I'd become adept at the Windows system used in the library and it was fast, like asking a person a question and you'd get it straight back at you – ok, sometimes the answer would be wrong but you'd just ask again in a different way.

"I wish they'd used these machines in my day," I'd often tell Claire, an old lady who'd taken up computer studies to fill in her days. I'd gotten used to sitting next to her in the library and we exchanged pleasantries; if I went to get a coffee I'd get her one and vice versa. A nice old lady but Greenwich was full of nice people, I suppose that's why I settled there.

I continued researching everything I could pick out of a history fifty years old. For someone like myself who'd gone through the processes of Auschwitz, I was uncovering more and more each day. It was like reading a book you thought you knew well, page after page then you turned another and found something new.

I'd need to interview Anatoly Mikhailov when I had enough evidence to prosecute him so spoke with Oleg Valdemars, my police safety net. I knew taking the ex-Kapo from St. Peters for questioning would be so much easier with Oleg on board and we both agreed Mikhailov was a survivor –he'd probably talk to try and get himself a deal. I just couldn't afford for the Church to start with the conjuring tricks.

Being retired seemed a long time ago. Luiza was supportive and the children just let me get on with it; they knew I was going to do it with or without their consent and had made the decision to help me.

Luiza kept notes on all the Kapos and, importantly, everything new that raised its ugly head. She was very organised and actually did what she promised, saving me a hell of a lot of time.

I spoke with Aleksy when I thought I'd possibly got enough on Schaefer, which if I'm honest was months later. I'd fended off his demands not realising his health was deteriorating. Naturally, he wanted to see the case brought to trial whilst he was alive and was annoyed with me, but I'd expected that. I'd pushed for delay for months, not understanding the time he'd granted was time he didn't really have – only I had the luxury of that. He didn't sound good, his language was slurred and his patience thin so I decided to go see him. "Let me come and visit you and I'll let you know everything. I think we've enough to prosecute," I told him.

"Ok, come next week," he offered.

I thought it best with his health deteriorating and though I didn't know how much, he didn't sound right.

I took a shuttle to the airport as Luiza needed the car for another of Lena's appointments with the dentist. She said she'd pick me up on the return leg. I'd used Jayride before, they provided me with a driver called Karl who was pleasant enough and he'd drop me outside my terminal at JFK for another long flight.

Aleksy was still staying at the San Georgio in Naples. I'd booked my own hotel, not far away, not wanting to be living 'over the shop' as it were, and when I got there I needed a long soak to ease just about everything I had. Room service had brought me a sandwich and I'd utilise the mini bar to relax. Falling asleep in the bath had become something I'd started doing in my old age, the cold water waking me close to midnight.

I'd arranged to visit Aleksy the following day, so I read over my notes contemplating the next move. The good news was I believed I had enough on

Schaefer to prosecute. The bad? I had to find him. I had no idea of his whereabouts or if he'd changed his name. Once he'd left Auschwitz, he just seemed to disappear. Although officially listed as presumed dead, Simon Wiesenthal had attempted to locate him in the '70s so I figured maybe he'd known something the rest of us didn't.

I decided I'd re-interview Ludek Hulka. I thought he accepted me and was more likely to let slip information the others wouldn't. I knew Aleksy wouldn't be happy with this, another delay, but I also knew quite well that under police investigation Hulka would have a lawyer and that would be the end of the matter. We had Ernst Schaefer in our sights and I felt Hulka possibly knew his whereabouts but once in the system and lawyered up I doubted very much they'd allow him to talk.

I approached the hotel with some trepidation. Knowing I was dealing with a terminally ill man who wanted to see justice, my plan may not seem to be achieving that goal for him. It was unfair, I knew that, but it would give us the best chance of catching up with Schaefer.

I entered and enquired at reception. "It's room 201 on the second floor, the escalator is just over there and you'll find his room just to the left of the lift as you exit it. I'll ring ahead and let him know your coming," he said. There was something in the receptionist's manner that made me think Aleksy was actually living there full time. I'd thought he was just vacationing. Taking things for granted was a mistake I'd made on many occasions and often it would be over the seemingly most obvious things. Over the years, I'd solved crimes by going back and picking up on the obvious; simple errors of judgement.

I knocked at the door half expecting to wait but it just clicked open. I entered to find Aleksy lying in a bed, nurses tending him.

"Hello, Aleksy. How are you doing?" I offered.

"I'm not too good," he slurred, struggling to talk. He didn't look too good either and I could clearly see he wasn't going to last very long. He'd created this whole thing and I doubted he would get to see the fruits of his labour. The nurses made their excuses and left us alone to talk.

I tried to get him up to date on all I'd found but I could clearly see he was struggling – a ventilator filled his lungs and then emptied them.

I decided to ask him what he wanted; he deserved that after thirty years, it was his project after all, not mine. I'd hoped to get Schaefer but I was no longer sure we had time. If we went straight for the Kapos at least Aleksy would see justice. He attempted talking.

"Ezra,..." he paused, swallowing spittle, it was slowly drowning him. "I know you want Schaefer....," another pause as he waited for the ventilator's cycle to allow him to speak. "I want him too... I've worked most of my life on this...," another swallow, I waited patiently. "But I realise... I couldn't have done this without you... so my decision is to let you do what... you want." He looked at me with sorrowful eyes, a man who knew his life was deserting him. I estimated he had days, maybe weeks if he was unlucky. Either way, it wouldn't be long before his body would lose the battle. I felt enormously sorry for him, this man I'd known briefly as a boy in Auschwitz, practically his whole life dominated by that evil place.

"You're a good man Ezra... I knew that back....," he coughed, starting to choke a little. I went to his side, to see if there was anything I could do. "Just sit me up a little," he asked. I understood; the saliva would be easier to swallow sitting upright.

"I'm going to die, Ezra," a short break as he gathered himself. "I've lived my life in the shadows....of Auschwitz. I didn't have a family," he told me. "They all died in that place... I never married after," he explained. "There's no one for me." He looked so afraid but I recognised it wasn't the approach of death that frightened him but that it would take him when he was alone with no family to comfort him.

At that moment, I realised that Auschwitz was going to take yet another victim if I allowed his life to end this way. I couldn't do that, he'd given me so much, so much to correct my life, to enable me to put my demons to bed. If it weren't for him, I'd have forever carried the weight of my past around with me silently strangling my heart. He'd allowed me to mourn the loss of my family and not hide away from that anymore. I was reborn in 1993, after receiving his letter, after years of hiding who I was, afraid to face up to my past, afraid of what it would do to my wife and children. I owed him so much. I hadn't known it at the start, and I believe Aleksy hadn't either, but he'd freed me from demons and the horrors that no one should ever have to witness. Aleksy Markowski, the little boy in Auschwitz who'd witnessed me extinguish the life of Jarmil Pleva, must have thought of me as his only link to his family.

"I'm thinking of staying for a while, Aleksy," I said looking into his eyes. "We'll do this together, my friend."

His eyes became wet and the tears rolled down his face as I held his hand and we talked about nothing in particular, the files put on the back burner for a short while whilst we both took time to realise who we were. Together, like brothers, we'd both been through hell and I wasn't going to let this 'boy' down.

I phoned Luiza that night after talking to the nurses. He had at the very most two weeks before it would take him. I told her to get a flight and join me, I was staying until the end. She understood my feelings and said she'd make arrangements the following day; she'd just need a flight, the hotel was a double room so she could easily be accommodated.

The nurses said Aleksy would likely succumb to respiratory failure. Hopefully, it would be in his sleep and peaceful, as some are. They were aware he had nobody, no family, and said he'd booked them personally, his financial situation enabling private nurses to tend to him 24/7 at this stage of his life.

I hadn't realised it, his behaviour was abrupt and conversations had been short when we used to meet but, whilst lying in the bed, he told me he was afraid of me – he was afraid I'd see the young boy in his eyes and afraid I would respond by looking at him as I had all those years ago with the eyes of a killer.

We sat talking for hours about our lives, mine with Luiza and the children, his mainly around his obsession with the files but I found he liked the New York Jets, the NFL a hobby of his. I told him I had a dog and recounted all Max's little foibles, how he'd bring a slipper to greet you at the door. "A burglar would be scared off by his ferocious bark," I told him, "but if they were brave enough to ignore that lion-like roar they'd find him on the other side of the door, a Labrador with a slipper in his mouth wanting to play." He smiled and looked up at the ceiling. "Thank you," he said. I knew what he meant. I didn't have to ask him what for, it was natural. I just pushed on with a story about my daughter as a youngster, the one where I thought I was being a good father sending her to self-defence classes, thinking she'd enjoy them, but apparently, it would overwhelm her when asked to stand and demonstrate a manoeuvre causing her on more than one occasion to yell at the instructor "Don't touch me! I can do it!" Again, a smile went across his face, he had a family now. My intention was to make him lose the feeling of having nobody, he had us as his family and he wouldn't go to his death alone and unloved.

I phoned Cooper Collins and Oleg Valdemars and told them to start the procedures needed to denounce the Kapos. Coop had been making contacts with the relevant Agencies on my behalf, his membership of the International Police Association coming in handy. I wanted it done so Aleksy could go in peace. I'd sort out the outcomes after he'd passed.

The exception was Ludek Hulka, I'd risk one Kapo to trap Schaefer. I'd thought hard about it but Hulka couldn't escape even if he wanted to. I'd try to interview him later but I'd tell Aleksy we'd got them all, he deserved the peace it would bring.

I hadn't planned on the possibility of Aleksy dying so suddenly. Although I knew he was ill, I'd not paid enough attention to it until it was too late. I'd buried my head in the work, allowing it to consume me and whilst he was fighting for life, I was ignoring his pleas for me to start denouncing our targets. To say I felt guilty for that was a wild understatement. I should have listened but I'm a pig-headed idiot at times and now he was bedbound. Yet another regret to cope with, the one of not getting there sooner; I may have been able to take him out for a day had I done so.

Luiza arrived two days later, it was as quick as she could manage. She kissed Aleksy's forehead as he lay there like he was family even though she'd only actually met him once before. I'd pre-warned her what to expect but, still, I could see she was moved at his condition. In such a short space of time, his body had turned enemy on him, refusing to recognise those connections from his brain that would allow him to do simple things like swallow. At this point, he was using a suction system to take excess fluids from his mouth to stop him from choking on them.

He could still talk and, although it was difficult, he wasn't giving up; his strength of character was enormous. An ability to endure was a hallmark of survivors and Aleksy was being tested to the extreme, but this test was only ever meant to be failed.

We had our lunch and meals sitting with my friend, he'd be fed by tube but he wasn't fazed by that, he just got on. We played some word association games and even when you thought he wasn't quite with you, he still was, sneaking out a pertinent comment. He asked after our dog and the children, saying I'd made him feel close to them over the days and that we'd spent some good times together during our visit.

He passed away on Tuesday, August 31st, 1994, the same date a complete ceasefire was declared in Northern Ireland and it struck me as fitting – harmony announced on the day a man, who'd been through more hell and misery than could be imagined, relinquished his hold on life. Almost a tribute, I thought.

He died peacefully, holding my hand, Luiza holding his other and he wasn't alone, he was amongst his family. Such a brave boy; somehow, he'd always been a boy in my eyes, ever since I found out who he was.

My upset was immeasurable, to me he was my last tie to my previous life – at least the last tie I wanted. Tears flowed down my cheeks and I couldn't stop the involuntary chest spasms. Luiza realised I was letting go and put her arm around me, cradling my head to her chest. He'd become a real friend in such a short time, we had a mutual kinship bound by trust and he'd given his life's work to me, trusted me with everything. His whole life had been dedicated to this and it took all he had.

The only thing this young boy could do when he left Auschwitz was to compile evidence against the perpetrators. He couldn't do what I'd done and put it away, his life was the whole process of justice.

He'd passed before we denounced the Kapos, so quick was his decline it just wasn't possible to put the wheels in motion fast enough to get things going. His last words to me were, "Don't let them get away with it. We survived, so many didn't have such a luxury."

Many people survived Auschwitz but not many dedicated their lives to finding a reason for what happened to them and who was to blame.

In his last days, Aleksy'd shown me photographs of himself when he was young, sent to him by a now dead distant relative. I recognised the face of the young boy and from then on I could see it in him every day, the boy he still was.

During this time, he said to me, "Emil, when you saw me?"

"When Aleksy?" I asked.

"When I was a boy, in barracks 10, remember?"

"Yes." I tried understanding where he was going with it.

"They'd taken my parents...I was hiding from them." He looked at me with tears in his eyes and I felt the guilt he'd carried all this time. Just a boy. The SS must have selected his parents for the gas chambers and Aleksy had hidden, scared as you would be, especially at that age. I'd disturbed him and he assumed I was there to kill him. It explained his fear of me. "It's ok, Aleksy, you were just a child, you couldn't have done anything," I offered him, but those tears showed me he'd suffered the burden his entire life.

His passing was a reminder of my life before, we were tied by fate but his life wasn't wasted because he'd done something special, something for the millions annihilated by the Reich. Giving his life to the cause of justice, he'd left me solely in charge of all of his files and work over the years – he had nobody else and I was proud he'd chosen me to fulfil his work.

The funeral was held in Italy and we stayed to pay our respects. I was surprised to see others there. Maybe he did have family I didn't know about but, after the funeral, I asked them and it turned out they were former colleagues from many years back. I don't know how they found out but they were welcome.

I made sure his headstone had the symbol of the holocaust survivor; he deserved that. It was a quiet ceremony and I felt a breeze in the trees like I'd experienced many, many years earlier. "Shhhhhh," they whispered as they welcomed my friend home.

A small bird sat on top of his grave. After all those years had passed, there he was, still watching over us, singing as before, seemingly pleased with himself. When he flew off into the trees, he was welcomed back from his performance – "Shhhhhh," they whispered again.

Aleksy Markowski had got my attention and I'd followed everything he'd tasked me with. I swore to him on his deathbed that I would conclude the files and bring justice to the millions deprived of a life. His was now over, our work was not.

Over the next few days, I'd find myself breaking down, out of the blue; the loss of my friend had opened up long-forgotten emotions. Luiza would let me be, she knew I had to get it out of my system but I had so much inside, I was an emotional wreck. To think I'd been able to keep all of this within for so many years astonished me but I was glad I could at last mourn the way normal people do. It helped, I must admit, but it was draining.

Tentatively, Luiza asked me, "Can you let me inside that box now?"

"In time Luiza, in time."

Aleksy Markowski was and forever would be a young boy in my eyes – even as an old man he'd always been that scared child who once asked me to "please, make it quick." I'd miss him.

Chapter 15
Karl Neumann

Losing Aleksy had hit me hard and my return to Greenwich came as a welcome break from the emotional roller coaster I'd found myself on. It had been exhausting but I didn't have time to relax, the Kapos were being arrested any day now, the process was happening.

Soon, they'd all be getting a knock on their doors and I wished I could be at each one but my job was elsewhere. I had to trust who'd been put in charge of the arrests to do their part whilst I took another trip out to Bucharest to visit Ludek Hulka. I had much to talk to him about and knew what I had to do, questions I'd need to build up to and, anyway, I'd get updates from Oleg Valdemars and Cooper Collins regarding the arrests and how they went; calls I was looking forward to with immense anticipation.

I arrived in Bucharest on a Friday night and I'd take five days, returning on a Wednesday. I read a newspaper on the plane, Muslim terrorists had kidnapped and beheaded sixteen Algerian citizens and it seemed the world had learned nothing in the past fifty years.

I visited Hulka after making arrangements with Marie, who'd by now had gotten used to my name. "Hello, Marie, I'd like to pop in and see Ludek tomorrow. It being a weekend, I thought I may walk him through the New Spring Cemetery?" It may have seemed macabre, taking an old man through a graveyard, but I'd read it had some wonderful headstones and was quite a nice walk.

"Hello, Emil. Yes, we often walk our clients in the park, as we call it. It's a lovely walk and not too far away. I'm sure he'd be happy to see you. I'll let him know you're coming," she confirmed.

I sat in my hotel room, going through my notes to remind me of the monstrous things he'd done so I didn't fall into the trap of feeling sorry for him. I also needed to remain professional, take myself out of the situation and rise above any emotions I was feeling. I was still just a detective getting information out of a suspect and I'd done that many times before but this was difficult, like interviewing the Devil when you'd grudgingly begun to enjoy moments in his company.

I had to ensure I got this right and kept my wits about me. I only had one shot and was aware if I blew it, and he realised what I was up to, I'd effectively lose Schaefer. I needed to be ready, any signs of recognition and I'd have to change tack and try again later when he'd forgotten what we'd been talking about.

I'd become aware that Mikhailov had more than likely killed my mother and sister and I readily admitted those feelings crossed over to all the Kapos, but with Hulka I was determined to listen and not react; just do your job, Emil, I told myself.

I arrived at the home at midday, thinking I'd give the staff time to get him ready. It had been a few months since I'd last seen him and I naturally wondered if he'd changed or deteriorated since my last visit. In fairness, I *had* thought the next time I'd see him would be in a courthouse but things had changed, we had an SS man to catch and my best chance of assistance, in reality, was a very old man with vascular dementia. I followed Marie up the stairs to his room, the day was gloomy outside but there was a chance of sun breaking through the clouds later.

I said hello. He responded, "Hello, how are you? Remind me, I'm sorry my memory isn't what it used to be."

Marie interrupted, "It's Emil, your friend from Czechoslovakia. You remember, Emil?" she said, unknowingly.

"Ah yes, Emil, take a seat. Marie? Can we have two cups of tea, unless you'd like coffee, Emil?" he replied, innocently.

I asked for a coffee. She nodded and disappeared out of the room and down the stairs. "Now, Ludek, how have you been, old friend? I've not seen you for a few months," I told him.

"I'm fine, apart from a few pains in my legs. I don't get out enough they tell me."

"Well, we can sort that out, can't we? What about a walk? I believe you have a wonderful local park," I offered.

"That would be nice. I think I've been there before. Marie will tell me when she comes back with the refreshments." He managed a smile.

We had our drinks and chatted about mundane things then set off for the walk, my mind on what I needed to do. *Get it right, Emil, don't mess up.*

"So, Ludek, what did you do when you left Bohemia?" I began the build-up, carefully step by step, going through the motions for roughly fifteen minutes attempting to make him feel comfortable before I tentatively posed the question that really mattered. "So, have you heard anything from Lukas lately?"

"No, not from Lukas," he replied, matter of factly.

"Have you heard from any of your friends lately?" I asked not expecting any joy but building up his confidence. He surprised me.

"Only Janis. He called recently."

It still shocked me that after all this time they'd kept in touch. "What did you talk about? Is he well?" I asked, trying not to sound as though I was prying.

"Yes, he told me he was well. He always calls me at the beginning of the month," he responded.

I wondered why he'd do that, what could he possibly need to contact Ludek Hulka once a month for? Was it regarding the distribution of money to an old comrade?

We walked and chatted and he seemed comfortable so, in between words of no meaning, I'd add a question and then another.

"So, have you heard from Ernst?" I said, eventually, nervous about what answer would come.

"Ernst?" he looked genuinely puzzled.

Maybe I'd got this all wrong, he didn't look like he knew an Ernst. In my head, I was screaming: '*All this work, the time I've put into this bloody file and he doesn't know Ernst Schaefer for God's sake.*'

Then he let out: "Ernst? The only Ernst I know is Ernst Schaefer but we haven't called him that since Auschwitz."

I snapped out of my displeasure. "Yes, that's who I meant," I said.

Why do you ask of Ernst?" he inquired.

I thought I'd blown it, he's onto me. "Oh! I just wondered how he was. I've not heard of him for a long time."

"Why not, Ezra?" he said, saying the name I'd been known by in Auschwitz.

I was definitely in unchartered waters here but he still looked confused so I calmed him down.

"Shall we have a cup of tea? Marie has given us a flask, let's sit down." He'd just admitted he knew Ernst Schaefer and I just had to be patient. I had to ensure I didn't scare him off and I knew through experience that inside his head he'd still be wondering. Although relaxed, with his tea in hand, his recognition and the name 'Ezra' would be too fresh in his mind so I decided enough was enough. I'd return the next day, give him time to forget so we sipped our tea and spoke of the flowers and trees before I said, "Shall we walk back now, Ludek? It's looking like rain and we haven't an umbrella but I'll come again tomorrow. I'm in town until Wednesday, so we'll take a walk again."

As an experienced officer, I knew not to push for information too soon, you can blow a whole case by seeming too keen and Ludek was a complicated nut to crack. If I'd pushed just one more question I'd have risked squandering the whole thing. I had to be casual, a slow build-up, each day going a little further until, hopefully, he'd reveal Ernst Schaefer's whereabouts. I knew he had what I wanted now, it was only a matter of time before he'd let slip something important.

I remember thinking I must tell Aleksy and then catching myself, forgetting he was no longer with us so I phoned Luiza and told her what I'd nearly done, she said it was natural.

The next day, we started over, once again with my prop in hand. This time, I brought apple tarts, freshly baked from the local shop, and we did small talk over coffee in his room. Eventually, in the cemetery, we got past the innocent pleasantries.

"So, have you heard from Ernst lately?" I enquired.

Momentarily, he looked puzzled. "Ernst? The only Ernst I know is from Birkenau and we haven't called him that for years. He changed his name after the war to Karl." The name was familiar then it hit me as I recalled in the file that it was his middle name.

Hulka had a mischievous look on his face. I thought he was playing games with me at first but he was enjoying the conversation. In his eyes, I could see something, a twist and he was smiling, no 'laughing' at me. "He's a new man now," he pronounced with a twinkle. He felt clever and I could see the inward smile come over him. We walked some more, sat on a bench, drank coffee, made small talk about the flowers and the weather but I was thinking all the time, 'new man'? Was he trying to fool with me or was he telling me something? 'A new man' in German was 'Ein neuer

Mann'. It didn't make sense. But he'd said it in a deliberate way as if sharing, yet not sharing, a secret. Then it occurred to me. 'Newman' was a common surname or at least 'Neumann' was.

Walking him back, discussing anything that took his fancy, I thought, 'I'll have another go at this tomorrow'. It was worth a try. I knew not to push too hard but I could change my approach and simply add in the 'fact' that I knew a Karl Neumann.

I took him back to the rest home and told him I'd see him the next day, like old friends meeting up. It was an act I'd gotten used to but I hadn't forgotten what this man had done or what his knowledge could reveal and I felt a step closer to a location, and maybe an address. The following day, I threw 'Karl Neumann' into the conversation and he'd accepted the name as someone he knew but he'd not reacted.

I was struggling to get the one thing that now eluded me but Ludek, at one point, had mentioned South America though I couldn't get him to clarify whether he was talking about himself or someone else; he'd been tired and had rambled a bit so I'd had to leave it at that. South America was a big place and I felt I was banging my head against a wall, trying my best but getting nowhere. When I next mentioned it, he was evasive.

That night, I phoned Cooper Collins for a favour. I asked him to conduct a search in countries like Argentina, Chile, Paraguay, Columbia or Brazil to see if anything showed up around 1945 for a Karl Neumann. It was a long shot but Coop's brother worked in Immigration so that might make liaison a bit easier.

On Tuesday morning, my mobile rang, it was Oleg Valdemars. "Hello, Emil. I'm just letting you know the arrests have taken place, all three have been detained. Lukas Baur put up a bit of a struggle, he's being charged with assault on three officers on top of the historical crimes. Janis Ozols came quietly. He didn't put up any resistance, he almost seemed to be expecting it, like he accepted his fate. He's been put on suicide watch. Now, Anatoly Mikhailov claimed he had immunity but the Church didn't have time to intercede, although we are expecting them to provide some representations. I'm sure we'll be receiving interference from them soon. However, I'm fairly sure we can fend all of that off, so don't worry. You've really done a great job on this case. We have virtually everything we need to get a firm prosecution. All the evidence is there, the files you've given are comprehensive and I give you my congratulations," he said.

"I can't take credit for that, it's my friend Aleksy Markowski's work. I just identified them," I offered up.

"No matter, Emil, you've both done a fine job, give him my thanks and congratulations," he said not knowing my friend had passed away. I didn't see any point in explaining.

I entered the home, again greeted by Marie. She offered a cup of tea before I saw Ludek, apparently he was bathing so I sat in the living room nodding 'hello' to some other visitors. When Marie returned, we sat chatting about Ludek, she wanted to know a little bit more about him so I gave her the basics, not the truth. I told her what I knew of his family background and said he'd been in Auschwitz, probably giving her the impression he was just an inmate.

"I find it interesting, all these wonderful places in the world." She saw my quizzical look. "Well, I know he spent time in Venezuela in the 70s, it must be amazing to travel like that," she said.

"Venezuela. Why do you say that?" I asked her.

"Oh, he often talks about it. He receives letters from a friend out there," she confirmed.

"Does he still have any of those letters? It's just they may be from a friend I know. We lost contact and it would be interesting to catch up," I asked.

She smiled. "I'm sure he'll have kept them somewhere in his room. They're from his friend, Karl."

This was the breakthrough I'd been looking for. Postal rules and regulations varied from country to country and I'd omitted to learn the Venezuelan rules but often they required a sender's name and address on the rear of parcels and correspondence. All I had to do was find the letters.

Bath time was declared over and now was my chance. I sat and chatted with Ludek for a while then took advantage of him paying a visit to the toilet, looking in all the most obvious places. Sure enough, in his bureau there they were, each one with a Venezualan stamp. I swiftly checked the rear of several; no luck, no name, no address. I could hear it wouldn't be long before he was back with me, toilet flush, tap running, door handle turned. I took one and stuffed it in my inside pocket, closed the bureau and returned to my seat just seconds before he came through the door.

Half disappointed yet still excited at the thought the details I needed would be inside, I gently inserted probing questions into the conversation but he wasn't responding how I'd hoped and when he began to ask questions about the 'old days' I made my excuses and left him for the last time.

Out of sight of the Baronesse home, I took the letter out of my pocket and scrutinised it. I slid it out of the envelope, three pages, the handwriting was what I'd describe as childlike, more like scribble than a grown man's though it was discernible in places and I could make out, "I look forward to seeing you." I checked the franking on the front. Smudged, but I could read the date '1992' and another number. It showed a recent connection between them and at least I had something. I wasn't sure but I thought the number might be a postal designation.

Only one thing I could do now, old-fashioned police work. I phoned Coop again and asked him if he could find me something out about the franked number on the envelope. He got back to me with the news it referred to the town of San Antonio De Los Altos. He'd anticipated my next question, "And there are eleven Neumanns listed in the phone directory; three with the initial K, before you ask."

Getting home, I returned to Greenwich library and my favourite computer. I paid to get birth dates from records and discovered only one person really fitted the age group I had for Karl Neumann. The staff were great and set me up with an email address. It was a good idea, one I hadn't considered, this way all I had to do was find a computer and I could receive messages and pictures wherever I was.

I dug a little deeper and found Neumann had popped up in the summer of 45 – probably through a 'ratline'– finding a haven to be able to live a normal life. I looked at other areas of the Nazis' escape to Venezuela and found the dictator Castillo had been trading some 73 tons of gold through the Middle East holding onto his power financially for years, there was a suggestion the gold was taken from the Jews – the fillings pulled from the mouths of Jewish corpses between the gas chambers and crematoria being one source. Newspaper reports indicated there was a current investigation working on that theme; one which would probably be defended with the actual finances being investigated.

Castillo had held this gold for many years possibly as far back as the war and it was looking likely, to me, that the escapees lodged their stolen cache in Venezuela. It occurred to me that perhaps Schaefer, or Neumann as I now believed him to be, was the only one who'd known the true extent of their pilfering. Having secured his future with Castillo, he'd then been feeding the others with the interest, giving all involved in the crime a good life.

But was Neumann the man who'd organised the theft of gold from Auschwitz? I was intrigued by the direction my investigation was going. Clearly, there were a number of Nazis who would have to have been involved in the theft of 73 tons of gold, surely Neumann couldn't possibly have done this alone?

According to my research, the Wiesenthal Center was looking into eighteen suspected Nazis in Venezuela and requesting the Government work with them to hunt them down. I'd phone the Center with a casual enquiry, see what I could find out, but my window of opportunity might be closing – should word get round in certain circles, I expected some of these names to disappear from public view.

Anyway, I had an address now for Neumann. San Antonio De Los Altos appeared to be in an area for the well-to-do, which kind of matched the profile I was looking for.

I'd seen him in Auschwitz, in the Kanada compound, but not frequently enough to be able to be certain I would recognise him, unlike the others he'd always worn a service dress cap and I never met him face to face. I knew him by reputation and from a distance. It would be interesting to find out what he looked like. A quick search provided many pictures but I deleted what was irrelevant and was left with two. Then I discounted one of them, printed off the other and called Coop again.

"Emil, you're a pain in my ass. Ok, there's something I can do but I'm running up a whole mess of owed favours here. I know someone in the FBI and they can maybe check with their Venezuelan contacts to see if they have an ID card photo or something else they can give us. If they manage it, I'm going to owe them big style so don't think you just get to walk away from it this time." He hadn't said 'No', so I was hopeful.

A visit to Venezuela wasn't something I'd planned to do but I'd information that had taken my interest and I had an internet photograph I wasn't sure of. To be honest about it, I knew I was going to have to go.

I spoke to Luiza who didn't want me to make the trip. "It's a dangerous country, you don't need to risk anything, just do it from here," she offered.

But I just had a gut feeling, a policeman's instinct you could call it and, although uncomfortable, by now I was used to the flights. I'd learned to take my Walkman, spare batteries and a few cassettes to kill time.

She dropped me off at the airport, telling me to be careful, "You're an old man now and vulnerable, watch your wallet and don't go down any darkened streets on your own," she told me, like a mother hen clucking over her chick and here I was being given instructions to look after my wellbeing, an ex-detective of many years service. I don't know what she'd been watching on TV but Venezuela was somewhere not to go according to Luiza.

I arrived at Caracas at 6 pm local time which gave me a space to get a shower and settle into my hotel before I grabbed a quick meal. My plan was to rent a car and travel to the address I'd found then I'd stake it out until I eventually had a visible sighting. I'd brought an SLR camera with a telephoto lens; there wasn't any other way to do this I thought, the risk was way too high, any hint of his recognising me and he'd disappear into the ether.

That first night, I took a walk after my meal and found a little place called the Living Pub, it was nice. I'd kept a newspaper from the flight and began reading it until I was rudely interrupted by some louts, one of whom had stumbled into my chair. My initial thought was they were just drunken youths until I saw the swastika tattoo. They were the kind of annoying types that needed their voices to be heard above all else. I decided to move on, my concentration had been disturbed. On my way out one of them stood in the doorway blocking my exit. "Excuse me," I asked. He just looked at me smiling, not moving. I noticed his friends were watching from the bar grinning and encouraging him. Again, I said, "Excuse me," adding, "May I pass by?"

"Excuse me!" he mocked, looking down his nose at me. "Jew boy, beg me and I'll let you pass."

I looked at him, not much of a man I thought, maybe eleven stone with no visible signs of muscle. Even at my age, I thought I could embarrass him but not the others, there were just too many of them but I wasn't going to beg. I'd seen the worst of life in my time, cowards of all kinds, and taken many a beating but clearly this specimen in front of me wasn't worth my effort. I put my arm straight and saluted. "Heil Hitler!" I heard their laughter behind me, the other thugs found it funny, so much so that the boy in front of me stood aside, embarrassed he'd made a fool of himself.

I'd had a lucky escape, it could easily have escalated. As fit as I was at my age, I was no match for a gang. I'd not tell Luiza about it, she'd have a field day with her, *I told you so*.

I got a call from Cooper Collins, he had information from Oleg Valdemars, they'd been able to hold Anatoly Mikhailov and the other three Kapos until trial. Ludek Hulka had been arrested and put under a watchful eye, his mental state had deteriorated rapidly upon arrest apparently, only to be expected now he was lawyered up. "Oh, and check your email. My guy came through for you," and he was gone.

I was pleased they were all in custody. The files Aleksy had put together over all that time would ensure a prison sentence, how long I wasn't sure but, at their ages, I was hoping for ten years – the death penalty was no longer an option so we wouldn't see real justice, just the version modern society believed in. I'd have loved to have seen all their faces as the weight of the law caught up with them, Lukas Baur especially, his bullying days over. He'd never see the outside of a cell again if everything went to plan.

That night, I said a prayer by my bedside, to all the victims of the camp. I hoped I'd served them well, Schaefer may well have changed his name but he hadn't changed who he was and I had a need to catch up with him.

I'd done night surveillance on many occasions so sitting in my hire car just down the road from the house was familiar territory yet this was different. There was an atmosphere about the place I couldn't put my finger on and I *needed* Neumann to be Schaefer more than I wanted it. I looked at my printed copy of the identity card Cooper had emailed me. I could see the resemblance to the photo I'd printed before. This one was more recent though because he'd had to renew his identification six years ago.

From a distance, I could see several cars parking outside his house, men in black suits exiting the vehicles. I'd not researched properly, how stupid of me, why had I not looked into this? He'd been a Nazi back in 45 but I never thought to look at what his hobby was now. It was a meeting, and clearly a meeting of the Fascist youth, that much was obvious. I'd read it was rife in areas of Europe and Venezuela had its own undercurrent but to witness a modern society acting this way was sickening. I wanted to get a bomb and destroy the whole building, these were National Socialists following the orders of the

Fuhrer in a modern era. Fifty years had passed and there were still such people in the world.

I sat in the car raging inside, only metres away from me was a meeting of the scum of the earth and I had to sit, watch and do nothing. But, my objective was clear, I had to identify Schaefer, nothing else mattered.

On the third night, around 8 pm, I was approached by one of the youths, dressed all in black with a shaven head, he looked more like a thug than someone with genuine political tendencies.

"What are you doing here?" he asked.

I made some excuse up about breaking down and waiting for a friend but I could see he was suspicious. His arm was exposed, deliberately I thought, to intimidate by showing the swastika tattoo.

"Don't come around here anymore. You're not welcome," he warned.

"Oh, I have no intention, I'll be gone as soon as my friend arrives," I lied. How was I going to identify Schaefer if I couldn't stake him out? He had people looking out for his interests and I hadn't expected that. In his 80s, he'd be an old man now but maybe the respect he received from the youth was due to the fact he'd actually been 'there' when they weren't even born.

I was being watched, I could sense it. I needed to get out of this situation as quickly as possible without blowing my cover. I lifted the hood of the car and made out I was fixing something or other. Then I started it up, got out, shut the hood and drove off. The Nazis had used youthful anger in their use of violence and I could see they were still using the same tactics. I'd return the hire car, it was of no use to me identified, sticking out like a sore thumb, so from now on I'd be on foot and in the shadows.

The following days, I sat with my telephoto lens and camera at a distance, hidden by trees. I'd surveyed the area and found cover, in the darkness of the night I sat fixed to my lens, a canopy of leaves disguising my presence. The house was no more than 100 metres away from me through the lens. I could make out everything I needed. It was now just a matter of time before I would get the vital evidence. In a way, it was exciting but also frustrating, I was in my 70s and doing covert surveillance, if Luiza could see me now she'd have a fit.

Rain fell around 9 pm but I had my foliage umbrella, the drops falling to the side of me as I scrutinised the windows and doors of Schaefer's house in the hope of catching a glimpse of him, ready to take the photographs that would be his undoing.

The door opened and six men came out, my camera silently clicking away at the profile shots. I'd got them, each one perfectly. More luck than photographic skills, I was pleased but then another man followed, looking left and then right. I knew Ernst Schaefer as soon as I saw his face, the camera clicking on sport mode, the roll of film spun and I quickly replaced it as he entered a car in front of the house and drove off, followed by his escort. I waited several minutes before I came out from my hide and walked back towards my hotel, pleased with the night's work.

The blow hit me from the left-hand side of my head and I went down to the floor, banging my arm as I fell, the kick catching me off guard and taking the wind out of my lungs. "Jew, have some of this!" as the boot caught me in the ribs. One after the other, the gang set about me, taking turns punching and hitting me like I'd taken many times before in Auschwitz. It was fifty years since my last beating, I'd been lucky as a policeman, self-defence was something I could handle but I was now an older man and six was odds I couldn't beat.

Blow after blow came at me as if in slow motion, the one to my eye came from a boot. I stopped feeling pain, the adrenalin kicking in to help me, words of hatred spat at me, ones I'd heard before. At some point, I realised I was in serious trouble because they didn't stop, they kept going until I felt something pop in my head and the next thing I knew I was coming to, people surrounding me. I looked for the camera but couldn't find it, my arms reaching out but it was gone. "Don't move, just stay still, there's an ambulance coming," a voice told me. I couldn't make people out, my vision had become blurred. I realised blood had got in my eyes so I wiped away the sticky liquid, feeling the bruising on my arm as I did so. My ribs hurt like hell, I thought I'd possibly broken a few, such was the kicking. Jesus, I thought, Luiza will go mental.

I became dizzy, light-headed, possibly the blood loss, everything became a blur and, at some stage, I blacked out, the light slowly disappearing down a tunnel in slow motion like a kaleidoscope – multi colours of the rainbow and then nothing.

Chapter 16

A Fight For Life

Apparently, I'd been in an induced coma for seven days. The beating I'd taken to my head had caused my brain to swell; the risk of losing oxygen to it persuaded the doctors it was best. I'd been brought to the 'Clinicas Caracas' and I spent several weeks there before I was well enough to be transferred home to Greenwich.

Luiza had flown out along with the children. The closing of my eyes by the kaleidoscope of light finally re-opened them and there I was, slowly focusing on the first thing I saw –my beautiful wife, sat in the chair next to me.

"Emil, oh Jesus, thank you! Nurse!" She ran off to get some help. Seconds later a nurse hovered over me briefly and eventually I could see Luiza clearly. "Hello you, how are the children?" I asked her.

"They're fine. Oh, Emil what happened to you? You nearly died," she said, concern in her voice, tears running down her face.

"Oh, I was jumped by a gang of young Nazis," I replied, trying to be nonchalant but then I remembered the camera. "My camera! Did they find my camera?"

"I don't think so but forget that now, it's not important, you've got a lot of getting well to do," she said in a half caring half telling off manner. I felt her disappointment in me, in my being so careless.

They'd almost beaten the life out of me, but the disappointment that hit me like a brick in the face was they'd taken the camera and its all important film.

Luiza sat with me every day and the children visited, I got a cuddle and a telling off from Lena but Daniel was oddly quiet, later he'd talk to me alone.

"Dad, you scared us. I don't say much but I have to tell you, Mum was beside herself. I've never seen her like that, I was so frightened. We thought you were dead. When you were in the coma they told us they didn't know what you'd return like." He broke down and wept. "I love you, Dad." His eyes full of tears, he could only let it out when the women had left for the canteen. I comforted him and told him I'd be alright, it was just one of those things, I could have been attacked anywhere. He disagreed.

"No Dad, you were jumped because of what you were doing." I didn't take the conversation further, I allowed him to let it out, he was a quiet boy but one who cared a lot.

That night, I lay in my hospital bed cursing my luck. I'd been so close to Ernst Schaefer but I knew I couldn't risk my life any more, I'd been lucky to survive and it wasn't fair on my family. I'd caught the Kapos, they were being processed, I could rely on the law to do the rest now and get my health back.

It would take me a long time to recover but I'd been through worse, much worse. The coma I'd been in had left me with a sore throat brought on by the ventilator – it was uncomfortable more than painful. The doctors told me my Coma Scale score had been seven and they'd been worried I'd experienced severe brain damage but I'd recovered well. I'd initially come out of the coma in what they called a minimal conscious state so I was a little lost in the first few days. I had to do some physiotherapy but my general good health had helped aid my recovery quicker than usual.

When I eventually returned home, I was fussed over more than was comfortable. My daughter moved into our home for a short while until I'd settled but I was getting fitter every day, although I was aware it had been a close call for a man of my age. I guess I just got lucky. God must have wanted me to see the work I'd done completed.

I did my physiotherapy at home, just general exercise, to build myself up and I had a few dizzy spells but nothing serious. The police investigation returned nothing on my attack, no perpetrators were found; they'd just disappeared from wherever they came. To be honest, I didn't really help the case.

Firstly, I was in no fit state, but mainly I didn't want to blow my cover with the research into Ernst Schaefer, although I had no way of identifying him now. I thought possibly another would, I don't know, maybe Coop or someone else. I wasn't really thinking too deeply about it at that stage. I really was being selfish about myself in the right way, I had to look after me now, I'd done enough. Aleksy would have been proud that all the Kapos were now imprisoned awaiting trial and even *he* would have praised me on doing a good job.

I actually enjoyed the peace of the recuperation and I started reading the books I'd been stock piling over the years. Luiza even bought me a home computer, connecting it to our phone line so we had access to the Internet. That was a wonderful gift, one that gave me hours of entertainment. I took up Italian. We'd promised each other we'd return to Sorrento, all those years had passed by and we'd often talked about it so I started a language course on the PC. It came with disks you loaded onto the computer but it was much more fun than just learning. If children could learn like this, I thought, it would revolutionise education – to make learning fun was a new thing, it had always been a chore in my life. I got myself a copy of Encarta, an encyclopaedia which loaded up with 24 floppy disks and took half of the computers space but it was fascinating.

All this was time at home, as Luiza wanted for me. She was worried about me going out but eventually Max wouldn't let me stay in. I couldn't make him suffer any longer, the poor guy. I admit I was a bit wary of my surroundings, a little nervous, but I never told Luiza that, I just got on with it knowing my confidence would return in time. I'd told victims of crime on many occasion the same thing, I had to take my own advice now.

Cooper would come around to see me with a case of beer and we'd sit on the porch drinking and talking over the cases. He emphasised to me clearly on several occasions, "They're bang to rights, case closed, Emil. You've no worries on that. They're never going to be released and, given their ages, they'll spend the rest of their days in prison."

Lena took time out most days to walk Max with me. It was nice. She'd changed a lot in her ways towards me, more caring and more understanding. I had no doubt before that she cared but in a different way. I suppose she'd thought her father was dead and the shock made her appreciate me more.

It was a good time, being able to relax with my family. We took days out and had fun. Luiza gradually forgot what I was doing over time, the memories fading, and after three months Auschwitz was out of sight – the cases still not at trial were biding their time to re-enter my life.

Max and I had a daily routine in the park. On my own, I'd think of all the things that had gone on. I thought about my life as a whole; one that was interesting to the outsider but full of hatred and chaos at times. I suppose I chose my working life but Auschwitz had simply happened. Whilst I did the thinking, Max sniffed a few trees, met some of his 'friends' and ran around like a dog possessed.

I thought of poor Aleksy, just a boy in that place seeing things death itself would fear, a life destroyed much more than mine simply because of his youth and how it had consumed him, yet that was what made him carry on. I realised not many survivors fell into the category of suicide, so precious they valued life.

I was contacted by a lawyer regarding Aleksy's will around this time. I was to go to an office to hear a reading of it. I knew already he'd left me the files, and I'd take a look at them at some stage, but for now my thoughts were really to just recover. I could read through those files at any stage. I really did feel that way. Coming close to death had concentrated my life and it made me take a very selfish view. Auschwitz could now be in the hands of others, I'd identified who I needed to – someone else could take on the baton as far as I was concerned.

When the date came around for the meeting, I really didn't want to go but found myself compelled to because of respect for my friend. Luiza came with me.

Haydn Noel was the lawyer and the meeting took place in New York so we travelled by train. It was Christmas time so we thought we'd take the city in at its best. Famed for its beauty, New York was quite stunning during the festive season. We'd be able to do a little shopping in Macy's on 34th Street and Bloomingdale's on 59th Street. Luiza would be in her element. I wasn't really a shopper so I tagged along, carrying things, making myself useful, but really it was for her. Our train journey took just over an hour, calling in at 125th Street station. A walk down Park Avenue took us in the right direction for the meeting and close to Bloomingdale's.

I was still walking a little slow, still not back to my fighting weight as the saying goes but I managed it. Not too far from Central Park, we arrived for the will reading around midday and were greeted with a handshake and an invitation to climb the stairs. In his office, he offered a coffee which we both took up before he went through the due process of telling us the contents of the will.

Aleksy had no family to leave his estate to. Obviously, the files were left to me but he'd left an instruction, a codicil, and Haydn explained that I was to be left a sum of money but it was given with a condition.

That condition took me by surprise and both Luiza and I had to think about what was requested. Haydn held some papers in his hands and told me they were just a selection from an archive that had much more information on war criminals, dossiers that needed my specific skills as a detective to investigate. I knew what Luiza was going to say so I said it before she could.

"Haydn, I'm grateful for the offer and I'll happily take the files but I've just spent the last three months recovering from a beating and a coma. I was assaulted by the sort of people you're holding in your hands," I said.

He nodded. "I get that, Mr Janowitz, but the codicil doesn't specify any time limit. It just says that you investigate further, particularly the case of Hertha Bothe, an SS Aufseherin camp guard at

Ravensbrück camp. She was also at Stutthof and stayed at Auschwitz temporarily in the February of 45," he explained.

"I understand, Haydn," I said, patiently.

"No, Emil, I don't think you do. You see, Mr Markowski was a very wealthy man, his books sold around the world in their millions and he'd invested well. He's left you a considerable amount of money," he said in a quiet, matter-of-fact way before continuing, "Herta Bothe was imprisoned after the war for war crimes and was released in December of 1951, it says here as an act of leniency. Mr Markowski wants you to look at Bothe's file, he says she's still alive and her crimes were never really investigated correctly. He believes you'll do it properly. She'll be coming up to 72 years of age now, so there's still time," he ended.

"Haydn, look, I appreciate you're just doing a job but my health comes first."

"Emil, your health will be well looked after because of this. You're being left over 14 million dollars and the codicil doesn't say you have to do everything yourself. You can employ a private detective to do the hard work. Simply put, Aleksy Markowski wanted you to take over control of his work, and only you."

I sat silently trying to take it all in. That amount of money would secure my children's future for the rest of their lives *and* the grandchildren we wished for. It wasn't easy to assimilate; besides, all that money and Aleksy couldn't save his own life.

"Jeez, Luiza, what do you say to that?" was all I could say.

Like me, she was in shock; neither of us had expected something like this. I thought I was here to collect the files or arrange their delivery so nothing could have prepared me for anything like it.

"I can employ a detective to do this? All I have to do is read and research the files?" I asked.

"Yes, that's about it. I'll leave you to talk for a few moments with your wife," he said, standing up and leaving the office.

Neither Luiza nor I knew what to say to each other, it was pure shock. Eventually, I said, "Well, that changes our Bloomingdale's shopping a little doesn't it?"

She laughed nervously. "Emil, should you accept, it will tie you to Auschwitz and there will be no end," she said and I knew what she meant.

As crazy as it may sound, it wasn't like we *needed* the money; our pensions kept us both well provided. It was more about our children and Aleksy's legacy – I couldn't just take this money and not create a foundation of some kind in his name. It could be a good thing if treated with respect. Maybe that's why my friend had done it, I was someone he trusted and believed in. I decided to ask for more time to think about it. Haydn agreed to my request. "Take your time, there's no rush, just make sure you're happy with your decision," he smiled back.

We completed our day and probably spent more money than we would have done in Bloomingdale's and Macy's but now it was money we could afford to lose if necessary.

Our return home on the train was one of quiet thought, both of us trying to think of reasons to take the money as well as reasons to turn it down. It was strange. I was still in recovery and it had been a chaotic period of my life, from a comfortable, nice retirement to a hospital bed in Venezuela. I think it was all too much and too soon, we both had to take a step back a little. We talked extensively together, we didn't involve Daniel or Lena, this was a decision Luiza and I had to make. We spoke of Aleksy's legacy and, if we took it on board, how we'd actually go about it.

Ernst Schaefer seemed a long time ago, he crossed my mind often and I did consider a private investigator could achieve what I'd failed to do. I suppose the ultimate decision was motivated by that if I'm honest. I knew Auschwitz wasn't ever going to leave my life and I balanced that off by admitting to myself it never had, I'd just attempted to hide it from everyone around me and, unsuccessfully, myself.

The decision was made together. Luiza told me she'd help me with whatever I needed to do and our first job after signing all the paperwork was to employ a private detective, we could afford that now. The process of finding and interviewing the applicant would be down to me.

I came across an ex-cop who'd settled in Greenwich but was hardened by the Bronx. Findlay Quinn was an Irishman, an ex-US Navy man and an old-fashioned cop I'd taken to straight away. We got on and he reminded me of myself in some ways. He understood the job in hand, accepted the terms and conditions Luiza had set out and his salary was good, better than mine in the last few years of my service but times and wage scales had changed.

Younger than me, Quinn would do the leg work on the cases that would unfold from the files I'd research; like I'd done for Aleksy. He'd be my eyes and ears on the ground.

We'd had a few beers together once the decision was made to employ him and I told him about the Ernst Schaefer case, copying the file so he could study it at his leisure. Findlay, as he told me to call him, was interested in the story. He couldn't believe Schaefer had escaped justice and he spoke his mind, which I liked. "Nách mór an diabhal thú," he said and then explained, "I'm sorry it means, aren't you the devil. I curse in Irish, it's an old habit." I liked that, the man had character. I was impressed with him, he was someone I could trust, a good choice and the fact Luiza liked him made it even better.

Following his appointment, I decided that until I'd read a little from the files on Hertha Bothe, I'd attempt to finish where I left with Ernst Schaefer. Quite simply, we just needed photographic evidence of him to start the full process. I sent Findlay out to buy a new camera and it was then I idly wondered what they'd done with the stolen one. Had they just tossed it in the river or sold it?

Ernst Schaefer had once again evaded capture. Was luck on his side or was it more than that? He seemed to have a lot of guards and people looking after him and I thought to myself, if you were in hiding, trying to make a new life would you be so open about being a Nazi? My research followed that line in the next few weeks. Was there something more to Ernst Schaefer?

I recalled my thoughts about all the Kapos living in capital cities. Why was that? I began making list after list, trying to make sense of all the information in my possession. I was missing something and I could feel it niggling away at me, something that didn't want to be found. I'd gotten so far with Schaefer but the door had closed on me in quite a violent way. I warned Quinn not to get too close and certainly to keep himself to himself; I didn't want a life on my hands.

He flew out to Caracas in late January, his simple mission to take photographs of everyone that entered and exited Schaefer's house. I received phone calls from him daily but the news wasn't good, the place seemed empty. He told me, "It's like he's on holiday or it's on lockdown." This was bad news, the kind you wished you were there to witness yourself but I'd made my decision, I trusted him and that was all there was to it. Disappointed as I was, I just had to accept it so I'd keep myself busy with something else in the meantime and see what I could turn up. One morning, Luiza came dashing into my study.

"Emil, your jacket, they've phoned from the dry cleaners."

"What do you mean, Luiza, what jacket? Calm down, what's the matter?"

"Oh, Emil, when you got out of hospital I put your jacket in the dry cleaners. I completely forgot about it, they've just phoned," she said.

"OK, then we'll go and pick it up, there's no rush." I said, with a chuckle.

"You don't understand. Emil. They found a roll of film in your inside pocket but the cleaning solution might have destroyed it."

The significance of what she'd just said struck me. Maybe all the kicks and blows had numbed my memory because I hadn't given it a second's thought. The roll of film! They'd stolen the camera but hadn't thought to take my jacket or check my pockets. Now, I remembered. I'd changed the roll for a new one not long before I was attacked, taken a few snaps and had sat there hoping for more. Could it be possible the film wasn't damaged? I had no way of knowing if it contained any evidence of Ernst

Schaefer, or Karl Neumann as he was now known, but at least intact I could take it down to police headquarters and have it analysed properly, see if they could rescue something. I wasn't trusting it to the local drugstore, that was for sure.

We drove to pick up the jacket and film roll immediately. On arrival, a lady handed over the coat first and started explaining how they'd gotten the blood stains out but it was of no interest to me and I interrupted, "I'm sorry, the film roll, do you have the film roll?"

"Yes, I don't know if it's been damaged but we can't be responsible..." she waffled on about their rules.

"Can you please just give me the roll of film? It's important," I again interrupted. She went to the side room and took it out of a drawer. Coming back she asked me to fill in a disclaimer, I just looked at her.

"I'll do it, Emil, you go off and try to get it developed," Luiza said, rescuing me from my 'moment'.

"Can you make your way home ok?" I asked.

"I'll be fine, go, Emil. Good luck," she said.

I drove to Greenwich Police HQ and found Cooper Collins. "I've a roll of film needs developing, Coop," I said.

"Holiday snaps go to your local drugstore, Emil," he said, looking at me with a tired face. I just stood, blankly holding the film in my hand.

"What is it?" he eventually said.

"This is it, Coop, the pictures I took. I had it all along, it was in my coat, I just forgot," I said.

"Ok, Emil, let's just get that down to the lab and get it looked at," he said, palming it from my hand.

"It's been in a wash, through dry cleaning of some sort," I told him.

"Jesus, Emil, you don't make the job easy, do you? Come on," he gestured to me to follow him.

The lab technician asked me what chemicals it had been through, "I don't know. What chemicals do dry cleaners use? I can get Luiza to ask, she'll have the phone number."

After a brief conversation with my wife, I put the phone down, "She'll phone me back." After a while,

Luiza called back, I'd have to return to the dry cleaners, the girl on the desk didn't know and the manager would be in at 4 pm.

"Hydrocarbons, Tetrachloroethylene, Glycol Ether, liquid Silicone and liquid Carbon Dioxide," Jane the branch manager trotted out. "Can you write that down for me?" I asked.

I gave the note to the lab technician who told me "Leave it with me, I'll do my best."

"It's very important," I told him, disclosing what it could mean so as to give him some urgency.

"Wow! It's not very often I get a job like this. SS you say? Give me twenty four hours."

I received the call the next day. It was all good, the reel had been treated with chemicals and saved, the pictures left were clear. I rushed down to the station to view them and there he was, Ernst Schaefer, no doubting the facial features of the man as far as I was concerned, but I needed something more. I'd sent an enquiry to the Simon Wiesenthal Center but they still hadn't got back to me. I just wanted whatever they'd got so I could be absolutely, no doubt whatsoever, sure. He was the one man I hadn't had close contact with and that fact was now creating a little pool of indecision in my ability to convince others.

News coming from Quinn wasn't sounding good but then again Venezuela was chosen by the Nazis for the exact reason we were now facing – it seemed extradition wasn't looking a likely option, Schaefer had connections going back a long way. We'd been close, almost within touching distance and the bastard was getting away with it. Positively identified, he'd remain in hiding in Venezuela like he'd done for nearly fifty years.

I lay the file and the photographs out on the table in my study and examined them for days, searching for another way, something I thought I was missing. Maybe if I looked hard enough it would appear but nothing did.

Chapter 17

Judgement Day

Findlay returned from Venezuela. I was working hard on the Hertha Bothe file, examining and collating evidence to use against her. We walked to MacDuff's, our local bar, and had a few beers; you could get a good meal there too so we took advantage of the situation.

"Emil, there's unfinished business in Venezuela. I'd like to go back. I understand the position we're in but I just think there's still a slight chance *if* I can get access to the right people," he said, whilst tucking into a Shepherd's Pie and a Guinness.

I agreed with my heart but my mind told me another story, I had reservations. I really admired his devotion; it was commendable so I didn't dishearten him after all he'd done for me. He knew what I'd been through and had become a confidant, listening to my stories of Aleksy, Lars and myself – listening to all the misery. He'd taken it all on board. In any case, what harm could it do? It's not like I couldn't afford it anymore and Aleksy would want me to spend his money like this, so I agreed. Findlay would return to Venezuela, one last attempt to convince someone in authority to extradite a war criminal.

He'd done a swell job for me, he was a good man. I could see that in people just as I could see the bad and Findlay had a good heart.

Anyway, I had Hertha Bothe to fill my time whilst Luiza busied herself founding a memorial for Aleksy Markowski. It seemed only right that the man who'd created all of this was acknowledged. She'd done a lot of ground work on it, something I wasn't good at but I gave her my support wholeheartedly.

Bothe had managed to avoid the death penalty, unlike her colleagues. Athletic in her youth, she'd spent time at Ravensbruck concentration camp and then went to Stutthof where her nature earned her the name 'the Sadist of Stutthof'. She selected people for the gas chambers personally. Her trial was never gifted the evidence it deserved and, somehow, she was given a sentence of only ten years compared to several colleagues who were hanged. As an act of misguided leniency, she was released in 1951.

This was what Aleksy wanted me to do, I understood this now. I had a natural interest to want justice served on people like this. As I unraveled the case, I received the remainder of the files Aleksy had worked on. It was staggering; I'd not be short of research. My friend had left me plenty to do, the incentive clear, do what I'd always done, catch criminals.

I had a meeting with Findlay when he eventually returned, yet again, from Venezuela. I thought he'd have no chance with the authorities and had begun thinking that kidnap might be an option as it had worked for the Israeli secret service, Mossad, when they took Eichmann off a Buenos Aires street. So much so, I mentioned it to him.

"You're right, Emil, there's just no way we can extradite him. Kidnap? It's a potential minefield. There's just too much risk involved," he replied, shaking his head. Disappointed as I was, I told him not to worry.

"You did your best, Findlay. I wouldn't ask you to risk everything, it's not worth it." I hid my feelings well.

He went quiet. It seemed like an age then he eventually dug into the satchel by his feet, dropped a newspaper on the table and said, "Emil, it's on my shoulders."

I picked it up. It was Venezuelan, a local paper, the headlines declared, 'Karl Neumann dead'.

He handed me an envelope. "You know I was in the Navy but I didn't tell you everything. I had some colleagues of mine take care of it; all ex-SEALs. They gave Schaefer a message before he died."

I stared back at him. "But, how do you know we had the right man? What if I got it wrong?" Suddenly, I was horrified in case I'd caused the death of an innocent man with my insistence I knew Neumann was Schaefer.

"You didn't get it wrong, Emil. I chased up the Wiesenthal people, used a few contacts. They trawled their records and came up with his identity card and fingerprints, the ones he had taken when he was posted to Auschwitz. We managed to get confirmation from a glass he used in a bar and then we double confirmed it after they killed him."

"You took fingerprints off his body?"

"Not exactly, there wasn't time. I had it done later, when we came back with his hand.

I was stunned. I waved the envelope at him. "And what's this? Is it a confession?"

He laughed. "No, Emil. It's the bill."

****

He'd woken up with the feeling that something wasn't right. Fumbling for the bedside lamp, he was suddenly bathed in harsh, white light. A voice said, "Ernst Schaefer. Aren't you the devil." Then, almost silently, bullets ripped into his body, blood seeping into the sheets and the mattress. As he lay there, fighting for breath, arms waving wildly for the emergency cord that used to dangle above his pillows, he felt the coldness of the silencer against his forehead and a voice whispered in his ear, "Nách mór an diabhal thú. The ghosts of Auschwitz say hello."

They exited through the security office, past the slumped CCTV operator and his relief, whilst the body of Karl Neumann swayed gently to and fro by his feet from the bedroom ceiling beam, blood dripping from the hole in his head, rivulets from his chest negotiating the contours of his neck and face.

Across manicured lawns, they disappeared into the darkness and scaled the protective wall, the bodies of two Dobermans and their handlers nearby. Minutes later, two cars glided silently down the slope, lights and engines coming to life only when reaching the junction a hundred metres further on. Parting left and right, later they'd be parked in a dimly lit side street in Caracas.

Chapter 18
The Little Bird

I'd spend many a year working on the files, bringing to justice criminals Aleksy had identified over thirty years. I enjoyed every moment. I worked closely with Findlay and not every file ended the way Schaefer's had but I'm not saying it never happened. Luiza went back to her retirement with enthusiasm and I spent my spare time, but not all of it, on Aleksy's files.

Let's say it had been interesting and fulfilling coming out of retirement. Aleksy Markowski had certainly gained my attention and I'd spend the rest of my life working on his dossiers. I'd live a good life and I gave back to the victims my time. I was privileged to do what I'd been tasked with and I felt the presence of my family every time I lifted a folder to address an issue. Auschwitz was part of my life, it had never gone away and, like Aleksy, it took its toll on me but with his help I'd found a way to live through it by doing what I was born to do.

I dreamt of my parents often after the Schaefer conclusion, just as I had before but this time I had something more to tell them. "You must tell your story," my father would tell me and I'd return, "Papa, I have. I'm an old man now and the world knows. We took them on and we won, Papa."

Little Anna held my hand whilst also holding Filip's, swinging between the two of us with her best shined shoes on, trying not to get them scuffed. Mama looked at me as she always had. "You're such a good boy, we're so proud of you."

Filip looked as handsome as he'd always been and my grandparents sat arguing as they'd always done. There were no guards anymore in my dreams; they'd all gone away, leaving me to enjoy my family alone. When I awoke, I'd always shed a tear but not in sadness anymore. I just missed them as much as I always had.

We'd been walking Max in the park, Lena by my side. As I entered the house, I didn't feel right. I must have overdone it, dizziness and a feeling of exhaustion sweeping through me. I made my excuses, telling them I needed to rest. The world started spinning around, the floor seemed to be moving, it was an odd feeling and nausea made me lie down. The bed seemed to float and, as I closed my eyes, inside my head something felt wrong. Luiza came in to check on me but I was unaware of her talking, her motions seemed silent but her face looked anxious and worried whilst I had a feeling of peace; a warmth that gave comfort.

I must have fallen into sleep without realising, tiredness overwhelming me. I dreamt of a little bird who sang and watched over me and I knew he'd been waiting.

EPILOGUE

I found myself in Auschwitz once again. How I got there I don't know. I felt strange, like life had not been real, it all seemed so distant, like a dream when you wake. I found I could lift myself up above the ground yet the prisoners around me seemed oblivious to my presence but I could see and hear them clearly. I ventured into areas of the camp I'd not been to before, blocks that were not for the general population and found some terrible scenes.

The faces were all people I knew or were familiar to me, even the emaciated bodies seemed normal. I found people in tears and attempted to comfort them. Time didn't seem to make sense anymore; Auschwitz was a place where it no longer existed.

I thought it was just me but I saw people who were there and others who weren't, they'd already passed away yet they existed together at the same time.

I held onto little Anna's hand, her mother took the other. I couldn't stop the process but I gave her some comfort as the Zyklon B entered her lungs, suffocating her. I held her and took away her suffering. She died with me, Mama likewise. Neither suffered, many others did, but I couldn't help everybody.

She'd never left me, her smile a constant in my life, a beautiful happy girl who made us all smile, so I smiled.

I visited many people, all of who were in a desperate state but I found Ezra Farber. He was lying on his bed, close to death, his body still able but his will had deserted. He'd lain down to die, his last wish to be again with his murdered family. It was imminent and I thought I could see a faint smile on his face. What could I do? I had to do something; he was too good a man to lose. People needed him. He had something about him, strength of character and a determination all but now gone. I had to give it him back.

We swapped souls that night as he slipped away. He'd not forget anything, all his memories remained yet also became mine, entwining themselves with

Emil Janowitz. It was easy, you got a chance to do a good thing once in your life and, for me, to take so much pain away from somebody was the right thing. I woke and though I felt strange for a while I got used to it quickly.

That morning I stood and watched them take Filip's body away on the cart with all the others. A cold stare caught my eyes. Briefly, I thought I knew him but turned away, there were things I had to do.

Books by
Jack Carnegie

The Sweet Water Tales series

The Blink of an Eye

Into the Blue

The Way Home

The Sikora Files series

The Auschwitz Protocol

The Architect

The Belsen Files

Printed in Great Britain
by Amazon